NON SEMPER FIDELIS

Non Semper Fidelis

by Sam Foster

FITHIAN PRESS, MCKINLEYVILLE, CALIFORNIA, 2016

Published by Fithian Press
A division of Daniel and Daniel, Publishers, Inc.
Post Office Box 2790
McKinleyville, CA 95519
www.danielpublishing.com

Distributed by SCB Distributors (800) 729-6423

LIBRARY OF CONGRESS CATALOGING-IN-PUBLICATION DATA
Names: Foster, Sam, (date) author.
Title: Non semper fidelis : a novel / by Sam Foster.
Description: McKinleyville, California : Fithian Press, 2016.
Identifiers: LCCN 2016022087 | ISBN 9781564745910 (softcover : acid-free
    paper)
Subjects: LCSH: United States. Marine Corps—Military life—Fiction. | Race
    relations—Fiction. | Soldiers—Fiction.
Classification: LCC PS3606.O77 N66 2016 | DDC 813/.6—dc23
LC record available at https://lccn.loc.gov/2016022087

To Sergeant Lawrence Ferguson and

Master Gunnery Sergeant Louis Roundtree—

two of the finest men I have ever known.

Contents

Flags 11

Hill Trail 14

Request Mast 26

Graduation 51

Close Air Support 55

Courts Martial General 68

Roundtree's Coming 107

California Dreamin' 131

NON SEMPER FIDELIS

Flags

IT WAS THE FLAGS that struck terror. They were small—no more than a foot square—and white. Each had three blue stars stitched across the middle, and they fluttered gallantly from the front bumper of the General's car.

The small, wood-framed houses that lined the street were tidy, well groomed, and identical. That, and the fact that the area was bereft of trees or any large foliage that would have imparted a sense of grace, marked it as a place where generals and generals' cars didn't belong.

They knew why he was here. There was only one reason he came. Always the same reason.

The streets were normally full of life—the giggles and screams of small children and the bustle of women pursuing them or engaging with each other across the low cyclone fences that separated each house. But the instant the flags, and the car to which they were attached, turned off the highway and started slowly up the hill all life stopped. From the bottom of the hill to the top, the response was instantaneous. Not a phone rang; not a signal was given; but with absolute certainty, the women and the children froze, knowing death stalked here. There were no men to join them. Men may not have understood, or at least would have had to hear words of warning to know, but the women knew, and the children knew from the women. Besides, if their men had been here there would be no terror. That was their knowing. The General was here; one of their men wouldn't be coming home.

As the flags moved up the hill every heart above wished only that they would turn away. And the hearts below beat again, but they did not move. Death still hunted, but for someone else's man. It was those closest to the flags but still above them whose universe contained nothing else. In the still heat of the afternoon the only thing making the flags flutter was forward motion. As long as the flags' motion didn't fail before they passed, death called on another house. And so all they knew was the flags and their motion. Every strong eye strained for their flutter. The weaker—those with hearts unable to bear the luff of the silk cloth—looked away.

Until finally the gentle progress of the General's car slowed and it pulled to the curb. The flags drooped with condemnation. The driver's door opened and a big Marine in dress uniform, black bill of a barracks-cover pulled low over his eyes, stepped out. He walked around the car and opened the rear door. For a moment only a dark maw was revealed. Then a leg tentatively extended. It was covered with green gabardine pulled to a sharp crease and it ended with a black oxford shined bright to reflect the sun. A small, frail man rose above the extended leg. Like the driver's, his barracks-cover was pulled low, but three gold stars adorned his collar. He held his hands before him, palms up. On them lay a flag. It was perfectly folded into a triangle with only white stars on a blue field showing. The driver, rigid at attention, held the door. The General, worn small with his burden, walked slowly up the path toward the little wood-frame house where he would visit death today.

Hill Trail

THE OBSTACLE COURSE no longer held dread for anyone in the platoon—well, no one except Mueller. God only knew how that frail, four-eyed academic could be the product of three hundred years of Prussian breeding, much less the son of a Panzer Division commander, but he was, or at least claimed to be. They'd get him across today, because it was a team exercise and not even for time—at least the "O" course portion of the exercise wouldn't be. Jack would carry Mueller's rifle strapped across his back. Carter, who was even bigger than Jack, would strap Mueller's knapsack across his chest, and the other guys would push, pull, and lead Mueller up the rope ladder, across the swings and deadfalls, and even up the wall. Mueller hadn't made it over the wall in six previous attempts, but those had been individual. Even Mueller could pull his upper body up the rope with someone pushing his butt from below. Hell, if they had to the platoon would harness him into the ropes and pull him up. There was no time on this.

Clock or not, the new drill instructor was barking at them to move it. Corporal Hood was new to the company. He'd come in during the sixth week. Everyone guessed this was his first Officer Candidate class. What he lacked in experience he seemed to compensate for with bravado. He was a ball-buster.

Jack was the last one over the wall. He unstrapped Mueller's rifle and handed it to him. He was rewarded with a smile that was both embarrassed and genuinely appreciative. The other eleven guys were all squatted down in the shade of the wall.

"Sit, Kendrick," the DI barked with what Jack took to be a Southwest twang. Jack slid his butt down the wall and sat in the dust next to Carter. Even without the wall Carter would have given him shade.

"Listen up, shit-birds," Corporal Hood's high-pitched tenor commanded. "You're warmed up. Now here's the drill. We're going to run the Hill Trail."

The platoon gave a collective groan. The Hill Trail was three miles of steep, hilly woods that started at the end of the "O" course and quickly disappeared into the Virginia woods. It would eventually meander back around the Officer Candidate School compound and come out of the hills at the foot of the asphalt-covered parade ground, the "grinder." A final sprint of two hundred yards across the grinder would bring them back to the beginning of the "O" course and the end of the trail. In soft cover and shoes, dressed as the DI was, it could be a pleasant morning trot. But in hard hat and boots and with full kits and rifles, and with the mid-day heat and humidity, it could be a killer.

"Stop whining, ladies," he continued. "Here's the rest. We'll do it for time."

Kendrick shared a bleak look with Carter.

"Now the next part is special, so listen up good. The faster the time, the more points. Everyone who finishes with the platoon gets the points. You straggle, no points regardless of time." Hood paused for emphasis and looked right at Mueller when he continued. "Some of you can't afford to 'goose-egg' this. Some of you...Mueller...will wash out if you do. What will that famous Nazi daddy of yours say then, Mueller? Shit, he might be proud if his son gets to become a real Marine instead of a boot lieutenant."

Every member of the platoon looked straight at Hood so they didn't risk looking at Mueller.

"Now, shit-birds, here's the special part. The exercise is leaderless." He scanned all their eyes. "Understand?"

Canard, a thin, wiry officer candidate from Oregon, spoke up. "Would the Corporal explain what he means by 'leaderless'?"

"It means, Private Canard, that I will not be leading you. It means, Private Canard, that I won't be setting the pace or forcing the stragglers up. I'm just an observer."

"Who will?" The question rumbled out of Carter in a slow, deep bass.

"Whoever the hell takes charge. You fucking figure it out as you go."

No one spoke.

"Saddle up, privates." Hood pointed at the ever-darkening shadow that was the trailhead.

The only sounds were the rattling of gear as the platoon rose, swung packs and rifles into place, and pulled on helmets. Then a cough or two as the dust that rose with them was inhaled.

"I'm starting the clock...." There was a significant pause and then, "Now! Let's go, shit-birds."

The platoon crossed the open space before the wood and dropped into a slow, easy trot, with Canard taking the lead.

Jack nodded to Mueller to start in front of him. He and Carter brought up the rear. By the time he was started Canard had disappeared into the dark of the forest. He could still see most of the platoon. Corporal Hood was standing off the trail at the edge of the woods barking, "Come on, come on. Whoever finishes first is the platoon. You ain't with him, you're a straggler."

Jack rushed by him into the woods. The cool of the woods was instant and pleasurable, but within a few steps the trail started up steeply, and Jack had to raise his knees and drop his shoulders to keep pace. This running uphill in full combat gear was gonna hurt.

When he looked up his eyes had adjusted to the dark of the forest. It really wasn't as black in there as it appeared from the outside. The hardwood canopy hanging thirty feet overhead filtered out all but a very occasional ray of direct sunlight, and the ground cover of berry bushes and vines seldom gave a clear vision of anything more than ten or fifteen feet away, but there was plenty of light to see straight up the trail. And at this point that's what the trail was—straight up. After a while the trail curved gently up to the top of the first hill before it turned left and led along the ridgeline. The curves were slow and gentle, so on occasion Jack could see the entire platoon with Canard in the lead. Unlike Jack and the others, Canard ran with his back straight, even on the steepest part of the hill. He loped at a pace that suggested the gear bothered him no more than an extra two pounds of sand in his saddlebag bothered a favored thoroughbred in a handicap race.

They had almost reached the crest when Corporal Hood shouted, "On your left, Kendrick. I'm coming by."

Jack moved to his right to make way on the narrow trail and the DI sprinted past, knees pumping and white sneakers driving hard.

"Carter, move," the DI shouted again as he went by.

I'd like to race the asshole even up, Jack thought. *See how he likes it doing this with thirty-five pounds of gear and boots.*

Immediately before him all Jack could see was Carter's broad back in olive-drab fatigues. His black neck glistened with sweat below his helmet. His gate was a little crabbed and then Jack realized Carter's right elbow wasn't swinging back as his left foot strode forward.

He's pushing Mueller, Jack realized. He also realized the front of the platoon had crested the hill and life was about to get easier. Canard had slowed his pace so the head wouldn't get too far in front of those still struggling up the hill.

"Canard," the twang bounced down from above. "Is it true what I hear about you?"

Whatever Hood was after, he sure wanted everyone to hear.

"Corporal?" Canard followed Hood's volume.

"You ran track, College Boy."

"Cross-country," came the breathy reply.

"I heard you were good," Hood's voice echoed through the woods.

Jack crested the hill, and as the trail rolled to the left and headed down the soft shoulder of the hill his body straightened and his stride lengthened easily.

"Third in last spring's NCAAs," came the proud reply.

The trail twisted and now Jack could no longer see them.

"And this is as fast as you can go?"

Oh, shit, thought Jack.

"Carter...I...I can't keep this...."

There was labored breathing in front of Carter that Jack could hear almost as clearly as he could hear Hood and Canard.

"...up."

"Gawd damnit, Mueller. You gotta."

"Carter?" Jack found it hard to speak. The trail was turning up again. Jack could see the sweat fly off Carter's cheek as the broad black face turned toward him.

"Have Mueller unsling his rifle," Jack puffed. The pace seemed not to have slowed at all since they started back up the hill. "And let me by."

Carter nodded and turned back. "Okay, Prussian, can you keep moving and pull that rifle off your back?" And then he moved to the right.

Jack pushed hard to increase his pace and drove by Carter. Mueller was holding his head low and staggering a bit as he twisted the strap of the M-2 over his head.

Jack ran beside the rapidly tiring Marine and took the rifle in his right hand. He could see the green fatigue uniform of the next candidate less than ten yards in front and worked on catching him as he slung Mueller's rifle across his back. It would not slip past his own, and grunting he pulled it back off his shoulder to loosen the strap.

Behind him Carter drawled, "Damnit, Mueller. We'll be done in twenty minutes more and your daddy be proud."

Jack slid the rifle strap over his head and then grabbed the stock and forced it behind his back. The strap rubbed his neck until he wrestled the collar of his fatigue blouse under it.

"On your left, Jensen. I'm coming by."

It took him five minutes to work his way to the front of the platoon. Canard still led with Hood just off his shoulder.

"On your left, Corporal Hood. Comin' by."

Both Hood and Canard turned their heads in startled surprise.

"Canard," Jack grunted, "you gotta slow down. Guys are falling out the back."

"Canard, you don't need to listen." Hood shouldered his way up and ran beside Jack, behind Canard.

Jack twisted to look at the DI running beside him. "With all due respect, Corporal, you're an observer here."

Hood's blue eyes snapped fire. Jack eased a few inches to the right. The butt of his rifle and the barrel of Mueller's both hit the drill instructor, forcing him off the path and making him jump up on the hill.

Jack grabbed Canard's shoulder. "Slow it, Canard. There's no point."

Canard let himself be reined in but said nothing.

Hood staggered back onto the trail, forcing Jack to the left.

"Kendrick, what the fuck is that on your back?" Hood grabbed the barrel of Mueller's rifle and pulled.

Jack gave a violent twist to his shoulders to wrench free

of Hood's control. "M-2, Corporal. Found it on the trail." Jack
flashed his best toothy grin. "You might like to carry it. Makes
this whole experience much more challenging."

As he spoke Jack realized they were running in full sunlight. The woods had given way to a meadow extending a
quarter-mile across the top of the hill—the last hill, Jack knew.
Across the meadow, down one last hill, which would open up
to the grinder and then to the end of the course less than a
mile away.

The trail ran almost straight across before disappearing
back into the woods. Dust was still up on the trail from the
previous platoon in the exercise, and through the haze Jack
saw the dark green uniform of a running Marine fade from
sunlight into shade.

"Canard, you see that?" Hood twanged. "You can catch
'em, Canard. You can lead the platoon and run them down."

Jack saw Canard's back straighten even more and he
knew he was about to lengthen his stride. "Don't, Canard," he
pleaded. "If you push it that hard we'll lose Mueller for sure.
Maybe Jensen."

Canard turned his head to look behind.

"Canard, he's right." It was Schwartz right behind Hood,
his New York accent sharp and abrasive to Jack's ear. "Just hold
steady. We're fine."

Hood muscled past Jack and ran beside Canard's thin
form. "If four-eyes can't keep up he doesn't belong."

"God damnit, Canard, don't listen to him. Mueller's going
into intelligence, for God's sake. He only needs to be smart
and commissioned."

Schwartz's nasal tenor demanded, "Don't do it, Canard."

Hood matched Canard stride for stride, leaned toward him and said, as softly as labored breath would allow, "It's never been done before. No one's ever passed the platoon in front. We'll..." he puffed. "You'll be a legend."

Canard stretched up to his full height.

Jack pleaded, "Canard, don't."

He was gone. His heels threw dust behind him and he streaked forward and disappeared into the black of the woods.

Hood slowed and shouted back over his shoulder, "Who's with Canard?" And then even louder, "You're with him or you're a straggler." He gave Jack a toothy grin.

As Jack ran by him and into the cool of the woods he could see Mueller being pushed by Carter halfway across the meadow. He turned to face the trailing Schwartz. "I gotta stop him."

Schwartz nodded.

"You go help Carter and keep Mueller coming as fast as he can." He huffed some more. "No matter what."

The New Yorker observed their common plight. "You don't hold him, Kendrick, I'm fucked. You know that."

"I'll hold him," Jack assured, and then added, "The platoon—the whole platoon—will finish this together."

Schwartz stopped and turned on his heel back toward the meadow. Jack ran pell-mell down the rapidly descending and darkening path. It serpentined down a steep wash toward the bottom. Jack scurried around a switchback and could see Canard fifty yards in front and two S-curves below. He was running almost flat-out, his heels seeming to bite into the dirt with every stride.

"Canard," he bellowed down, "Slow up enough so at least some of us can finish together."

The Marine slowed enough to look up. "Who's coming?"

"Schwartz is right behind me. Couple of others."

Canard continued to run but not full speed. Jack could see his silhouette backlit by the light rushing up from the end of the woods.

He caught Canard just as the trail opened onto the grass. The grinder was one hundred yards before them. The last man on the leading platoon was just striding onto it.

Jack grabbed Canard's shoulder. "Slow it, hoss. They're coming."

Canard looked back up the trail. Hood's sneakers flashed specks of white out of the dark colors and were coming fast. The others were still dull forms well above him. Canard looked back at the grinder and the increasing space developing between him and his quarry.

He looked stern. "Not fast enough," and turned for the final sprint.

Jack dug in and tried to keep up but was losing him. "Damn it, Canard, it's not about you."

But the speeding runner didn't slow at all.

As Jack sprinted the sling of Mueller's rifle dug into his neck. He pulled the offending thing over his head and held it in one hand as he raced. Canard was ten feet in front as they stepped onto the grinder. The leading platoon was fifty yards in front with two hundred yards to go. Canard seemed not to tire, his strides now full-length.

"Stop," Jack shouted, and he hurled Mueller's M-2 with all his strength at the back of Canard's fleeing legs.

It hit him full stride and he staggered two steps and fell screaming. Jack dove on top and pinned his shoulders, his face inches from Canard's.

"Now stay there, damnit."

"Kendrick, get the fuck off." Canard struggled but was too light to throw him off.

"Kendrick, what the fuck are you doing?"

He felt hands on his knapsack pulling him up and saw white sneakers by his head. He hung on.

"Let him go, Kendrick. That's an order."

"Corporal, is this leaderless or are you back in charge?" Kendrick shouted.

The pressure pulling him up released and his full weight flopped back on the squirming Canard. He twisted his head up to look into the glaring blue eyes of Corporal Hood. "Corporal Hood, the platoon will finish—all of us." He saw his platoon rushing from the woods, Schwartz again in the lead. From the end of the course he saw a captain and Staff Sergeant Clue running toward him. The Staff Sergeant and Schwartz arrived from opposite directions at the same time.

"What the hell is going on here?" the head DI barked.

Kendrick rolled off Canard and smiled up. "A struggle for leadership, Sergeant." Now all the platoon except Mueller and Carter crowded around.

"Private Canard and I have just agreed the platoon will all finish the exercise together."

"Then get it done, Private," Clue growled down.

Canard stood. Through the legs around him Jack saw Mueller stagger out of the woods. Carter, right behind him, again had Mueller's knapsack strapped across his broad chest.

Jack smiled up, "Yes, Sergeant," and started to rise. As he put his weight on his right leg he felt a rush of pain and heard himself scream as he fell. He started to rise again.

Clue was instantly on his knees beside him gently pushing his shoulders back down. "Lay still, son. We'll get help." Then he looked at Hood. "Corpsman up. Now!"

Hood nodded and took off at a run just as Carter and Mueller huffed to a halt beside him.

"You okay, Jack?" Carter's black face dripped sweat and showed no hint of a smile.

Jack winced and then smiled. "Okay now, big guy." Then to Clue, "Staff Sergeant, I'd like to finish this now—with my platoon."

"Stay still, Private. You're through for the day."

"Staff Sergeant Clue, we started this together, I'd like to finish it together. Carter and Jensen are good at that fireman's carry thing." He implored, "Please."

Clue nodded and stood up. Jack reached beside himself, picked up Mueller's rifle and handed it back. Carter unslung the additional knapsack and handed that to Mueller as well. Then Carter and Jensen kneeled on either side of him. He sat up at the waist and put an arm around either man's shoulders. They slipped their hands under his hips and rose as gently as possible. The twelve Marines slowly walked across the grinder to the end of their course.

Request Mast

THE SHEET WAS HEAVY, and it irritated every place it touched—the tips of his toes, his knee, his hipbone, his nipples, and even his forehead. The skin at the spot of each contact was annoyed by the woof and warp of the fabric that had worried his skin for too long—far too long. But he resisted removing it. To uncover his eyes would be to give in to wakefulness, to give up on sleep, or the fiction of sleep. He had not slept well for weeks. His unworked body didn't seem to need sleep and eventually accepted it no longer—rejecting deep sleep, restorative sleep. But his soul was deprived of restoration too and cried out for it. Restoration or escape—escape that only the sleep could provide. So he would hide under the covers and pay the price in irritated epidermal nerve endings and pretend.

"Kendrick, reveille." Doc's friendly voice came soft but insistent. "Gotta wake up now."

Lying flat on his back as he was, his arms folded across his stomach, the punch was easy to throw. He didn't have to turn or move in any way. And he could hear the target he couldn't see. The voice came from down low, close by his ear. All he had to do was make a fist and swing straight up. He couldn't get his weight over onto the hip so he could strike hard, but he could strike, and did. Straight up through the sheet.

Even as his hand connected with bone his eyes flooded with the incandescent light bouncing off the yellow tiles of the high ward walls. And he screamed as the force of his blow twisted the traction holding his leg up and out.

The pain was bearable and not blinding, an almost refreshing instant awaking from the misery of his pretense at sleep. He cut off the second scream forming in his throat even as Doc's cry exploded.

"Jesus, Kendrick!"

The young, clean, angular face of the corpsman stared down at him. Its expression was pained. Clearly, even then, it was not pain from the inept and puny blow but from betrayal. The anguish it expressed was melancholy, not malice.

"What the hell was that about?"

Now his wardmates, at least those with beds nearby weighed in.

"Good morning, Sunshine. Look who done woke up?" boomed the Lance Corporal in the bed next to him.

"Fight!" yelled someone down the ward.

"Dumb-ass, Doc here going to pound on that bad wheel of yours, you play rough."

"Fuck off. All of you." The young Marine pulled the sheet back over his head and tried to turn onto his side, and screamed again as the force of his turn pulled his heel out of the sling at the end of the traction.

"Oh, shit! Kendrick, stop it!" Doc reached forward and gently lifted the sling back into place and slid the rubber inflated donut under his heel. "You're going to damage yourself."

"What's going on here?" a strident contralto voice demanded.

Kendrick looked up, as a starched nursing cap atop a thick, curly, blond thatch appeared half a head below and between two Marines in blue bathrobes.

"You men move."

One stepped sideways. The other planted his crutches and scooted aside crab-fashion to follow the command, and the broad, low shoulders of Lieutenant Commander Ludwig forced through.

She planted her large, white presence beside his bed and stared unblinking across the form of the prostrate Marine. "Corpsman, I asked you a question."

"Nothing, Ma'am. Kendrick woke up screaming. That's all."

Kendrick lay rigid, at attention. Without rotating his head he turned his eyes to the speakers on either side of his bed. He looked at the officer now. Her jaw was clenched and energy crackled around the edges of her narrowly focused eyes.

"Corpsman, you lie to me and you're on report with him." She spoke deliberately. "Now what happened?"

He saw Doc struggle with his courage. He shifted his weight back on one foot as though to bolt, and his eyes looked down so he made no eye contact. After a moment he brought his balance back to the balls of his feet and raised his eyes to meet hers.

"Nothing, Ma'am. Kendrick's heel fell out of the traction and he screamed. That's all."

"Corpsman, I saw the entire incident, including the blow, from the nursing station." She looked down at the patient for the first time. "You're on report." Then she wheeled and strutted back to her glassed enclave.

THE dayroom was constructed of wallboard painted light green above the linoleum-tiled floor and below the windows that stretched from waist height to the peaked ceiling. The furniture, Naugahyde padded, curved stainless, provided an austere décor, but sunlight streamed in from three sides. That and the panoramic view of maples scattered over a wide, well-mowed lawn that rolled gently to the Potomac created warmth that belied the décor.

"You gonna play or your black Georgia ass just gonna sit there?"

"Shit, Nigger, why you such a big hurry to get beat?"

"That's Sergeant Nigger to you, Nigger."

"Who he! Look who's pullin' rank? Fergie, you all tense today."

"I ain't tense. I'm just tired of bein' propped up on these sticks waitin' for Country Boy to play. As for pullin' rank, I'll pull it on anyone in the place any time I want 'cause I'm the ranking fucking Marine on this motherfuckin' ward!"

"Okay, Sergeant Nigger, trump." Country Boy threw down the three of spades. "Game and rubber. That how they play bid-whist in New York, New York?"

"She-it! You had it. I lost count."

"Now, will you sit your green, Navy-issue pajamas, and your blue, Navy-issue robe and your black ass down. And for Christ-sake relax. What you so tense for anyway, Ferguson?"

He sat down and pulled a pack of Lucky Strikes from the pocket of his robe. "Who got a light?"

"Catch, Fergie," a voice boomed from near the door, and a silver missile thrown hard streaked toward him.

Ferguson's hand shot up and then stopped dead, wrapped around the lighter.

"Whee-ew! Man's still got hands."

"Just no wheels, no more," Ferguson grumbled. He lit the cigarette and lobbed the lighter back toward the door as he exhaled a stream of gray, sweet, pungent smoke. "Any of you know what the ruckus was at the other end of the ward 'bout reveille?"

"That what's eatin' you?"

"Nuttin' eatin' me. I just asked."

"Nuttin' for you to worry your pretty head about, Fergie, but it was kinda fun."

"What was?" Ferguson asked.

"One of them shit-bird, college-boy, officer-candidate, drop-out pukes hit a corpsman."

"No shit. Which one?"

"Svobodny. Doc Svobodny."

"No asshole. Not which corpsman. Which Marine hit 'im?"

"Them pukes ain't Marines. Can't even figure why they put 'im here."

"Where you think they otta put 'im?"

"With officers. Not Marines."

"But they ain't even officers. They dropouts. They ain't got no commission."

"They're Marines, damn it. You might not like 'em, but they're Marines," Ferguson insisted. "Which one was it?"

"The one with a leg strung up like a harp. Not very fuckin' smart, you ask me. All Doc's gotta do is backhand that pin stickin' out his leg and shit-bird screamin' for morphine."

"Doc ain't gonna hurt 'im."

"How you know?"

"'Cause he's Doc, asshole. Ain't gonna hurt nobody," Ferguson said. "Why'd he hit 'im?"

"Shit, beats me. No one knows. Doc don't know. Shit-bird ain't said. He just hit 'im."

"How long's he been like that?" Ferguson asked.

"Like what?"

"Strung up like a harp, asshole."

"Still testy, Fergie. Smoke ain't calmed ya?"

Ferguson exhaled and then ground the half-finished butt into the aluminum ashtray. "I ain't testy, and I still want to know how long Kendrick been here."

"Who?"

"The Harp; Shit-bird. Name's Kendrick. Private Kendrick, USMC."

"Jesus, you do have on your stripes today. Well here's some news for you, Sergeant. Your shit-bird Private gonna stay that way a long, long time."

Ferguson said nothing and waited.

"That Nazi cunt Ludwig saw it all and wrote shit-bird up. He's gonna get busted and he ain't even got a stripe to give away. That leg of his ever heal, he sure as hell ain't goin' back to no Officer Candidate School. He gonna get to be a real Marine after all."

"How long, asshole? How long's he been like that?"

"Couple of weeks before the big bird brought you here from the Nam. First of April, give or take."

"So three months. My Marine's been hangin' there like that for three months."

"Yeah, something like that. What of it?"

Ferguson didn't reply. He closed his eyes for a moment, pushed himself up to standing, balanced on one leg and pulled his crutches from where they lay against the arms of the chair, propped them under his arms, and leaned forward.

"Where you goin'? We got us a rubber match."

"Later. I gotta go see the Doc." He swung his good leg forward, landed on it and hobby-horsed through the door of the dayroom and down the ward.

"DOC?" Ferguson stood leaning forward on his crutches at the door of the nursing station. He was looking at the back of Svobodny's head. It was uncovered and his black hair, made shiny with pomade and combed back, was about all Ferguson could see of him.

The young corpsman spun around on his stool and gave a smile of recognition. "Hi, Fergie. What can I do for you?"

Sergeant Ferguson made a point of appraising the young face closely. "That a mouse I see under your eye?"

"Ah, shit, Sergeant, cut it out. He didn't hit me hard enough to hurt anything 'cept maybe my feelings."

"So you okay."

"Sarge, about all Kendrick hurt was himself. I'm fine."

Ferguson nodded. "What happened?"

"Christ. Beats me. Kendrick had the sheet over his head at reveille. I went over to wake him and he swung at me. From under the cover no less."

"You didn't do anything?"

"Said, 'Kendrick, reveille,' and he swung."

"So what did you do then?"

"You mean before or after I put his heel back in the traction swing?" Svobodny smiled at his own joke and then his face got serious. "Ludwig saw it. I tried to cover but she wrote it up. Bitch," he muttered.

"You tried?"

"Sarge, I ain't puttin' nothin' in the nursing notes. She can write up what she wants. Nuttin' happened." Svobodny's jaw muscle bulged and his lower jaw protruded.

Ferguson smiled. "You're a Marine, Doc. Thanks."

"High praise, Sarge. Thank you."

"Where is she?"

Svobodny pointed across the hall. "Office."

"Thanks again, Doc." He swung one crutch around to go.

"Fergie," Doc's voice beckoned him back. "I thought Kendrick was my friend. He won't talk to me. If you find out why will you tell me?"

Ferguson looked at him. The muscles in his face were relaxed and his eyes unblinking. "Doc, you ever feel like you had to hit someone? Anyone?"

The young corpsman stared at him for a minute and then nodded.

"You are his friend, and now he's embarrassed. That's all."

— • —

HE knocked sharply three times.

"Enter," a firm contralto called back.

He had to use the crutch to hold the heavy door and crab in sideways. It slowly closed behind him. The Lt. Commander's office was small. She was seated behind her desk, which was positioned directly in front of the door. A straight-backed wooden chair in front of it was the only accommodation for visitors. High bookshelves along both walls were full of neatly arranged rows of medical texts and Navy manuals. Closed venetian blinds covered the sole window, directly behind the desk. A bland yellow light from above reflected off the walls.

Ferguson stood as erect as his crutches and bad knees would let him. "Sergeant Ferguson requests permission to speak."

Lt. Commander Alice Ludwig peered at him over her reading glasses. "Sit down, Ferguson."

He stared fixedly at the spot on the venetian blinds just over her head. "With all due respect, Lieutenant Commander, I'll stand. And it's Sergeant Ferguson."

She dropped her glasses from her face to the blotter on her desk and firmed her jaw. "As you will, Sergeant. Permission granted. And be brief."

"Lieutenant Commander, I understand you put one of my Marines on report."

"Your Marines?" she exploded. "Who the hell do you think you are?"

"I am the ranking Marine at this duty station." He stared, more rigid now—straight enough that his crutches were of no further support. They were only things he held trapped between his arms and his ribs. "As such, authority and responsibility for these men falls with me."

"Your duty station is my ward, Sergeant; your man is my patient, Sergeant; your Marine struck my corpsman, Sergeant. And yes, Sergeant, he is on report. Is that all?"

His right knee hurt, but his belly was full of adrenaline and he was alive. "No, Lieutenant Commander, that is not all. I am here to request that the Lieutenant Commander allow the chain of command to operate, and until such time as a superior NCO arrives, give me permission to handle discipline on the ward, like any other ranking NCO in any other duty station in the entire United States Marine Corps."

She looked hard at his eyes. "You and your Marines are TDY to the Navy. The Navy runs this hospital and you'll do things the Navy way. Permission denied. Dismissed, Sergeant Ferguson."

FERGUSON again stood in the door of the nursing station propped forward on his crutches.

"That was quick," said Corpsman Svobodny.

"Doc, do me a favor?"

"If I can, Fergie."

"Get me an iron and some Brasso."

"When?"

"Now."

"Ten minutes, Fergie."

"Thanks, Doc. Oh, Doc, one other thing. Get me a cane, would ya?"

WHEN Corpsman Svobodny stopped by Ferguson's bunk fifteen minutes later the Sergeant had just closed his footlocker and was stuffing it back under his bed. Neatly laid out on the bed were a pair of dress green trousers and a blouse, a web belt with brass buckle, black oxfords with a can of shoe polish and a rag beside them. A small wooden box sat on the pillow.

"Getting dressed for parade, Fergie?"

He smiled up. "Something like that, Doc. Got the goods?"

"All here." Svobodny laid a varnished wooden cane across the end of the bed. He set a small blue and white can with a red screw top beside it. When he dropped the iron on the bed cover the entire mattress bounced. "Drop the iron off at the nursing station when you're done. The rest is yours."

"What do I owe you for the Brasso?"

"Compliments of the US Navy, Fergie."

Ferguson started with the shoes. He wound a rag tightly around the index and middle fingers of his right hand, rubbed the covered fingers lightly across the polish and then into a cup of water. With his shoe shoved onto his left hand he rubbed the wetted cloth in a small circle around the toe of his shoe until the polish was gone. And then repeated the process again. And again. And again, until he could see his freckles and the nap of his short hair in the surface of the shoe.

The greens were next. After opening the metal door in the wall next to his bed, he let the small ironing board drop out. He pressed a sharp crease in the trousers, smoothed the blouse of wrinkles, and lastly pressed a sharp front and rear into the cloth "piss-cutter" he'd pull down low over his forehead.

The Brasso cleaned the tarnish from the belt buckle in minutes. Range qualification medals in rifle and pistol and campaign ribbons were last. They only needed to be dusted and pinned on properly, the Bronze Star superior to the others, even the Purple Heart.

When he was done he folded away the ironing board,

stripped his robe and pajamas, and, for the first time since the mortar hit him, put on his suit of honor.

"She-it, Fergie. Where's parade?"

Ferguson smiled and said nothing. He slid the piss-cutter onto his head and tried the cane. He thought his good bad knee would hold. He stepped off onto it, cane in the opposite hand. It held. Sore, but it held. He rocked over onto his bad knee as he stepped forward, sure to plant the cane firmly beside it before he eased his weight onto it. He rocked far to the side, but it held, and he pushed back up with the cane. He grabbed the iron in his other hand and started off between the rows of beds that lined the ward. As he hobbled toward the nursing station, he passed the beds of the injured officer candidates— the shit-birds.

"Why you up to all dressed for parade, Fergie?" one called.

Without looking he responded. "Off to do a thing the Navy way. And it's Sergeant Ferguson to you, Private."

For the third time this afternoon Ferguson stood in the door of the nursing station. "Here's your iron, Doc. Thanks." He laid it on the desk.

"Welcome, Fergie. You going where I think you're going?"

"Maybe."

"Don't do it, Fergie. She's too damn tough."

For the first time all day Ferguson laughed. Not a chuckle, but a big laugh that lifted his face, took away the care, and let him look as young as his twenty-three years. "You ain't been in-country yet have ya, Doc?"

Svobodny shook his head.

"She ain't nearly so tough as Charlie." And he turned to go, cautious of his weight.

"Fergie," Svobodny called after him.

He rotated his head so Svobodny could see his brown eyes.

"I was watching you come up the ward. Change that cane to your good side so it reaches out like a tripod with your bad leg. You'll rock less; won't hurt as much."

"Thanks, Doc." He turned, put the cane in his other hand, and stepped off.

HE knocked sharply three times.

"Enter," the same firm contralto called back.

He threw the door open with both hands, held it open with one and, cane in the other, stepped inside. Lt. Commander Ludwig was still behind her desk.

This time he was in uniform and covered so he observed the convention. Cane in left hand and standing at rigid attention he said, "Sergeant Ferguson requests mast."

THE corpsman stepped out of the nursing station with afternoon meds. He approached Private Kendrick almost deferentially. "Private, you interested in a little pain medication?"

Kendrick turned his head and looked blankly at the corpsman. "Yeah, Doc, I'm interested."

The corpsman took a small paper cup off his tray and extended his hand. Kendrick took it, and the corpsman reached for the glass on Kendrick's bedside stand and handed that to him as well. The patient swallowed the pills and washed them down. He then handed the paper cup back.

"Thanks, Doc."

"You're welcome."

They exchanged looks but neither spoke. Svobodny turned to go.

"Wait, Doc. Please."

He turned back.

Kendrick gulped again. "I'm…sorry, Doc…. Please forgive me."

The corpsman's face beamed. "Me too. Nuff said."

"I can't explain, Doc. I…I don't know…I don't understand."

"Oh, I do."

"You do?"

"Sure. Sometimes a guy's gotta hit something. That's all."

Kendrick blinked several times and nodded. "I guess."

"Only next time, the pillow, okay?"

Kendrick smiled until his teeth showed. "Promise, Doc." And he extended his hand.

Svobodny shook it and, smiling, turned to go.

"Hey, tell me one thing before you go," Kendrick asked. "What was that with the Sergeant in full parade dress a minute ago?"

"You know Ferguson?"

"Never met him. I've seen him back in the dayroom with the black guys playing bid whist. Saw him box a couple of times. Crutches under his arms, feet planted, and knocking snot out of guys forty pounds heavier than him. Lightning-fast hand. That's about it. What else?"

"Know how he got here?"

"Scuttlebutt is a mortar in Nam took out both his knees."

"Yeah, that's right. He'd like to re-up and go career if we can fix his knees so he's fit."

"Can you?"

"No."

"So what happens then?"

"He's out. Back to New York I guess."

"New York?"

"NYC. Downtown. The Avenues. You know it?"

"No."

"Very rough place. Projects."

"So what's a guy with no knees do in a place like that? He get a pension?"

"Buck Sergeant. Six years in. What's he get for his knees?" Doc answered his own question. "Not much." Then to Kendrick he asked, "What will you do?"

"You'll fix my leg, right?"

"We'll fix it."

"Contracts up, I'm out. No bars for me. I'll take my newly minted honorable discharge, my diploma from a nice private school, and go get rich. Assuming I get that honorable discharge."

"You'll get it. She can't fuck with you that bad."

"What about a guy like Sergeant Ferguson? What's he do, Doc?"

"I hear he's a legend in the projects. Maybe that helps."

"Legend?" Kendrick looked surprised.

"Story the bid-whist crowd tells is that at fifteen he was so fast with a knife his set called on him for fair fights."

"Fair fights?"

"Yeah, when two sets wanna fight but don't want to do the whole Sharks and Jets thing. Just two guys. Your champion and my champion," Svobodny explained. "Heard he was nineteen and O before he turned seventeen and enlisted."

"So what's our champion all tricked out about today?"

"I think I'll let Sergeant Ferguson tell you that himself."

— · —

"YOU what?"

"I repeat, Ma'am. Sergeant Ferguson requests mast."

"You've been watching too many movies, Marine."

"Lieutenant Commander, are you denying my request? Because if you are, I assure you, Ma'am, I will go from here to the XO's office and repeat my request with the addition that you refused to pass it on."

She sat well back in her chair and studied the face and form of the saluting Marine standing before her.

It seemed to Ferguson that she was seeing him for the first time.

"At ease, Ferguson."

He tried to spread his legs into the at-ease position. His bad knee felt like it might collapse, but his only concession was to hold his feet close together. He still folded his hands into the small of his back.

She motioned to the chair. "Sit down."

"With all due respect, Lieutenant Commander, I will stand. And my rank is sergeant and I insist on being addressed as such."

"All right, Sergeant, with whom are you requesting mast?"

"The commanding officer of this unit. That would be the Hospital Commander if I understand Navy protocol, Lieutenant Commander."

"You do, Sergeant." She smiled now as she looked up at him. "We can work this out, Sergeant, you and I. It need go no further than this."

"Does that mean, Lieutenant Commander, that you will give me the permission I requested?"

"Don't be unreasonable. This is my ward. I command here."

"Then we cannot."

She glared. He looked straight forward. Lt. Commander Ludwig picked up the receiver to the telephone on her desk.

"Wait in the hall, Sergeant."

He turned slowly and exited. Once in the hall he was relieved to rely heavily on the cane. Both his knees throbbed. He kept an eye on the door. When he heard it creak, he raised his shoulders erect, looking at the door. She held it open with one hand.

"Do you know where the XO's office is, Sergeant?"

"No, Ma'am."

"When the hall ends turn left to the elevator. Third floor, go south. Last door on the right. You're expected."

He turned to walk the corridor. He didn't hear the door shut and so walked very erect. Slowly, but very erect.

He located the Executive Officer's door with ease, knocked, and upon receiving response entered. A Senior Petty Officer sat at a desk to the left, guarding the only other door.

"Sergeant Ferguson?"

"Sir."

"It's Petty Officer, Sergeant, not 'Sir.'"

"Petty Officer."

"Sergeant, Commander Johnson will see you as soon as he's been able to review your book. We've sent to the ward for it, but you arrived first. If you'd care to sit?" He pointed to a wooden straight-backed chair across from the door.

"Thank you." Ferguson and his knees would be grateful for the relief.

He took the offered seat and managed to keep the sigh less than audible. Time hung heavy. A young corpsman Ferguson didn't recognize came in from the hall with a stiff manila folder more than an inch thick in his hand. He gave it to the Petty Officer without comment or recognition and departed as unannounced as he had entered. Ferguson controlled his impulse to scowl.

The Petty Officer rose, picked up a file, knocked on the door beside his desk and entered without any recognition Ferguson could hear. He was out again in less than five minutes.

"The Commander will see you."

Ferguson rose and entered. The XO's office was larger and better lit than the others. There was a picture of President Nixon on the wall. An officer dressed in whites rose from behind the desk as Ferguson entered. He was covered. Ferguson stopped and came to attention as quickly as his knees would allow.

"At ease, Sergeant."

Ferguson again came to the best approximation of parade-rest his knees would allow.

"Do you prefer to sit, Sergeant?"

"Thank you, Sir, I'll stand."

"As you prefer. I understand you have requested mast with the Hospital Commander."

"That is correct, Sir."

"Sergeant Ferguson, I've reviewed your file. You've served your country with distinction and honor. I trust I can continue to count on those virtues?"

"Sir?"

"Sergeant, this is a hospital. The commanding officer is a

doctor. I am not. His job is to deal with the issues that create best medical care for our Marines. Mine is not. My job is to deal with the usual command structure issues. Therefore, I hope and presume you will agree to deal with me."

"Sir, have you talked with Lieutenant Commander Ludwig?"

"I have."

"Then you know my request?"

"To have disciplinary command over the orthopedic ward."

"Correct. And to deal with the Private Kendrick situation."

"Sergeant, I understand your efforts here. Personally, I find them noble. But we have a hospital to run here." He paused and gave a gentle smile. "Ferguson, I also know the nature of your injury. You must be in pain. Please, sit down and let's discuss this." He pointed to an upholstered wing chair.

Ferguson pulled his spine up and brought his feet together. His hands came from behind his back with the cane in his left and his right with fingers folded together at the seam of his trousers. "Sir, Sergeant Ferguson requests mast with his commanding officer."

"God damn it, Ferguson, you stop this toy soldier shit now or I'll..."

Ferguson cut him off. "SIR! I will see my commanding officer as per Navy regulations or by tomorrow night Congressman Adam Clayton Powell of New York will know this Marine's lawful request has been denied."

The XO's lower jaw came loose and his face drained of color.

Ferguson maintained his salute and said, "And respectfully,

Sir, I've been yelled at by DIs who are tougher than you in your wildest dreams."

THE Captain's office was a mess.

Disheveled stacks of papers covered his desktop, poured over the edges, and pooled all around the floor along with puddles of medical journals and texts. In the middle of the chaos stood an aging Captain with strands of thin, gray hair extending at oblique angles from his large skull. His pronounced belly stretched the blouse of his whites to partially cover his belt buckle. He peered pleasantly over Franklin glasses at Ferguson as he entered. In response to Ferguson's attempt to bring himself to attention he extended his hand toward the one chair in the room whose seat was not piled with clutter. "Ferguson, come in. Sit down."

The Sergeant stood at rigid attention. "Sergeant Ferguson requests permission to speak, Sir."

The Captain swept a book from the seat of a straight-back chair and sat down. He smiled gently, "Ferguson, you have all the permission you want, but I won't stand on formality even for a United States Marine requesting a 'hearing before the mast' with his commanding officer." He again pointed at the chair. "Now, son, if you want to talk, sit down." And then added, "Please."

Ferguson dropped his salute and slowly took the two steps to the offered chair and eased down. After placing his cane against the arm of the chair he found himself sitting almost knee to knee with his commanding officer and looking into quiet, gray eyes that peered back at him.

"How can I help you, Sergeant Ferguson?"

"Sir, we have a problem with the Marines in the orthopedic ward and I'd like to fix it."

"Johnson briefed me. Chain-of-command thing."

"Yes, Sir." Ferguson instinctively sat silent waiting to see what the Captain would reveal.

"Ludwig can be...." He seemed to search for the right word. "Troublesome."

For the first time Ferguson smiled—a small conspiratorial smile, but a smile nonetheless. "Yes, Sir. She can."

"And that creates a problem for me as well."

"How's that, Sir?"

The Captain looked away—up toward a spot on the ceiling. "Rank has two functions in any military organization—competence and command. In the Marine Corps rank serves both masters." The Captain brought his gaze back down and looked directly at him. "You're a rifleman, Sergeant?"

"Yes, Sir, a grunt." Ferguson smiled again.

"Sergeant, huh? You run a platoon. Couple of three-man fireteams."

Ferguson admired the insight from a Navy man, and a doctor no less. "You understand our structure very well, Sir."

"Been around you jarheads for over twenty years. I've picked up a little." He paused. "So you, Ferguson, have two jobs. First is to have the professional skills to effectively lay down fire from your several teams. The other is to keep all those young Marines in line. That right?"

"I've never broken it down like that, Sir, but that's right."

"Navy doesn't do it that way, Ferguson."

Ferguson arched an eyebrow quizzically in response.

Again the Captain looked up toward the spot on the ceiling.

"Around here rank is far more a mark of professional competence than anything else. Sonarman's supposed to interpret clicks and clacks of sound bouncing around under the ocean. If he's First Class that means he's damn good at it. But it doesn't mean he's skilled at commanding men." His eyes darted back down to catch Ferguson's. "You with me here?"

Ferguson nodded.

The Captain maintained eye contact. "The command function in any Navy unit is assigned to someone who's good at it."

Ferguson nodded again. "That silly Master-at-Arms thing you do. Never did understand it."

"But now you do. You're TDY to my command so I can use you."

Ferguson leaned forward.

"How about I make you Master-at-Arms of the orthopedic ward? Problem solved?"

"Yes, Sir!"

"You still have to report to Ludwig, but discipline is your problem. Can you handle her?"

"Piece of cake, Sir."

"For you maybe." And now it was the Captain's turn for a conspiratorial grin.

"One other thing, Sir. The Kendrick issue."

The Captain rose and walked to his desk and picked up the only file not in a larger stack. The file was labeled, "Kendrick, John C." He handed it over. "Open it, Ferguson."

He did. The top item clipped on the right side was dated today. It was Ludwig's Incident Report.

"Please hand me the Incident Report, Sergeant Ferguson. I'll need to study it. Please return the file to the ward office."

The Captain bent down to a large stack of papers beside his desk, and raised the corner of the pile and slid the report on the bottom. "If she asks you or me, the report is on my desk for review and recommendation."

The Captain stood again. He was directly in front of Ferguson's chair. "Is there anything else you wish to discuss, Sergeant Ferguson?"

Ferguson rose, took a moment to compose his balance, and then drew himself to attention. "Sir."

Slowly the Captain brought his large rotund body erect. "Dismissed, Sergeant Ferguson."

THE profundities of Sun Tsu exasperated Kendrick. For Christ's sake, advice to take the good ground and leave your enemy the bad didn't seem worth getting famous for, even to a wannabe Second Lieutenant.

"AT-TEN-SHUN!"

It was barked in three staccato syllables, and with the instinct of one of Pavlov's dogs he responded. The book dropped to his chest, his arms extended along his sides and good leg flat and straight. It took a millisecond. Almost as quickly he was embarrassed that he'd gone for someone's gag and bent to the sound. His eyebrows arched and his lips pursed into a smirk, and he stared into the hard face of a "lifer" NCO.

"I told you to get at attention, mister. Now do it."

He did, and as quickly as the first time. His eyes fixed on the cords of his traction. There was no sound. He knew he was being studied by Sergeant Ferguson and could guess that the rest of the ward waited in silence for the drama to unfold.

His peripheral vision on the left registered the shadow of

mass and he felt the warmth of Ferguson's breath on his ear.

The voice whispered in a barely audible and menacing tone, "Do you have any idea how close your young ass came to a major fuck-up, Marine?"

He needed to look. His hearing couldn't tell him if this was real or if he was just being played with, but his vision would. He rolled toward the sound.

"Don't you look at me," the voice barked.

Kendrick righted his neck and studied the traction again.

"And answer my question."

"Does the Sergeant mean that I have not fucked up majorly?"

There was no answer, but he heard the scrape of a metal chair across linoleum beside him and then a soft exhale as the Sergeant made himself at home. The silence continued.

"At ease, Private." It was spoken softly.

Kendrick exhaled and relaxed his limbs. He struggled to turn away from his bad leg and look toward the voice. Ferguson had turned the back of the chair to him and was seated with his arms folded across its top.

"Kendrick, I've taken care of the Lieutenant Commander's report. Your book's clean."

"Thank you, Sergeant." He meant it.

"But there's a price. Do you know what it is?"

Kendrick studied the still brown eyes. They were too deep, and gave no clue. He shook his head in response.

"You deal with me from now on, not the Navy. And Kendrick, you don't even want to think about fucking with me."

Kendrick said nothing.

"Understand?"

"Yes, Sergeant."

Sergeant Ferguson stood very slowly, picked the chair up by its back, twisted it out of his path, and stepped past Kendrick's bed.

"Sergeant," Kendrick beckoned him back.

Ferguson stopped and turned toward him.

"Thanks, Sergeant."

Ferguson grunted in response and turned away.

"Sergeant Ferguson," Kendrick called again.

When the sergeant turned his head he continued, "Did you really have nineteen 'fair fights'?"

Sergeant Ferguson grinned. "Kendrick, you play bid-whist?"

"Something like bridge?"

Ferguson smiled and nodded. "You give me ten minutes to get this gear off and then have that corpsman push your bed down to the dayroom. I'll introduce you to some Marines."

Graduation

FOUR-HUNDRED AND TWENTY-SEVEN of their nation's finest stood ready for review. Six companies in ordered ranks—tall, straight, and proud. Each individual among them the standard of his nation's longest military heritage, and each ready to accept the obligations that would come with being named Second Lieutenant of the United States Marine Corps—obligations to forgo personality for Corps, to fight and die, to order others to fight and die. At rigid attention the sharp creases of their green gabardine trousers snapped in the Virginia breeze. The mid-day sun glistened off the mirror-high shine of eight hundred and fifty-four black oxfords and four hundred and twenty-seven black-billed barracks covers, each pulled so low not a single eye could be seen from the reviewing stand that they faced.

In front of each company stood one young Marine dressed

in the gift of dress-blues. The barracks cover was white and the drab green gabardine blouse of the others traded for a blue serge jacket with the mandarin collar, and the trousers of white worsted with a two-inch ribbon of red down the outside of each leg. This was the company guidon. He was the individual selected as the best among his fellows, the one to follow. And to reward him, and to display his excellence to those who might be too ignorant or indifferent to understand, and to make him easier to follow, the guidon, like Joseph, was given this wonderful coat. He also carried the company standard—the flag of the United States of America festooned with Marine Corps and company pennants at the top of the staff.

In the clear still of the afternoon the guidon of each of the six companies held these symbols low, at half-staff, and stared straight forward and fixed at some point beyond the boundaries of today's ceremonies. They stared past the reviewing platform with the assembled dignitaries seated there, and past the grandstands set up behind the platform. Had they not focused beyond their current reality they would have seen the two Marines by the grandstand steps. One, a private, sat in a wheelchair; the other, a sergeant, stood beside the chair, leaning on a cane. The grandstands themselves were full of well-dressed and ever-so-proud family and friends. These were the family and friends of the four hundred and twenty-seven—mothers and fathers, brothers and sisters, fiancées and fraternity brothers— all assembled to honor and commemorate this great passage in the lives of the four hundred and twenty-seven. It was the passage which for some would be the gateway to self-recognition and greatness, and for some the passage to eternity. They would have also seen the reviewing stand with folding chairs on which the dignitaries sat. Among those seated there, they might have recognized the Colonel who commanded Officer Candidate School and perhaps even the General who commanded MCB Quantico, Virginia. Most of the others of various ranks and in various uniforms they would not have recognized. Nor would they have recognized the couple seated in the front row on the General's left. Seated motionless as though holding themselves with a palpable tension. Seated with their feet flat on the floor and heads as erect as the Marines before them. Seated with the black cloth of their dress marking them with a formality that exceeded the occasion. The guidons would not have recognized them, but they would have known who they were. We all knew who they were.

As the guidons held their flags at half-staff, three mournful notes from a solo trumpet pierced both the air and their hearts with the first bar of that musical command used to pronounce the end of the day for a military unit or the end of days for one of its members. If the four hundred and twenty-seven had been rigid except for their breathing before, now even that rhythm stopped.

Thirteen weeks ago, the four hundred and twenty-seven had started as six hundred. As the days and weeks passed, their number had been reduced—eighty-two by resignation, fifty-eight by deselection as unfit, twenty-nine by hospitalization, three as Absent Without Leave, and one, Private James Robinson of Grinnell, Iowa, by death.

Jimmy had been assigned to "C" Company. He hadn't been the most fit guy at OCS, but he'd seemed okay—a bit overweight or at least flabby. If he'd been an athlete you suspected he'd never made varsity and hadn't done much physically his last couple of years in school. He didn't run well. At least not over distance. Jimmy had fallen out on the hill trail. It was one of those exercises run by everyone in the battalion—one company after the other. Those were always rough on the stragglers because the following companies had to get by them or risk being slowed. No one ever really knew if Jimmy fell off the side of the trail or if he was pushed. But whichever it was, when he went down, he'd had his helmet unbuckled—probably wasn't as uncomfortable that way, but it did make it harder to keep on. Jimmy's fell off as he rolled—they found it twenty yards uphill from his body. He'd rolled down the fall line far enough to bounce past a couple of trees. When his head hit the rock that stopped him, there was enough brush between his body and the trail so you couldn't see him from above. The autopsy said he probably died instantly, but who really knows? The guys in "C" Company knew he was gone, but not where—no one saw it happen. That night at roll call his bunkmate covered for him with a muffled "Yo" when "Robinson" was called. He even messed his pillow around in the bunk so it looked like Jimmy wasn't AWOL. But he couldn't cover for him at formation the next morning. They found him by ten hundred. Word was the ants had eaten his eyes out by then.

As the last note of "Taps" ended the Colonel rose and stepped to the podium at the front of the reviewing platform. There was a microphone there and he gave a short eulogy and observed what a fine officer James Robinson would have made. He then turned toward Mr. and Mrs. Robinson holding a plaque he'd taken from the podium. Mr. Robinson rose and as the Colonel handed him the plaque the sun glistened off the brass bars of a Second Lieutenant.

Close Air Support

EVERY NEWLY MINTED second lieutenant in the United States Marine Corps went to one of two duty stations. If he was a flyer, he went to Pensacola, Florida. All the others went to The Basic School—TBS to its intimates. If Officer Candidate School's function was to find which candidates had the desire, courage, physical skills, intelligence, and, most important of all, strength of character to be Marine officers, it was The Basic School's function to teach them how. If every Marine is a rifleman, then every Marine officer must be an infantry commander. Later they may learn artillery or intelligence or even logistics; but at their core, everyone is a captain of riflemen in assault and defense or he is not a Marine officer. Officer Candidate School taught him nothing of command or tactics. He learned the rudiments of those at TBS, and the consequences of inattentiveness, or lack of aptitude, were death—potentially his own, but even more important, those of good Marines. The Basic School's mission was to prevent that loss.

TBS was home, at any given time, to over a thousand second lieutenants and the officers who commanded and instructed them. In addition to students and instructors, TBS also included Headquarters and Service Battalion—H&S, as it was known. The Marines assigned to H&S supplied two essential, but widely divergent, services to the lieutenants. They provided room and board, and they also provided an enemy force against which the lieutenants could test the theoretical classroom exercises of battlefield X's and O's on the chessboard of the Northern Virginia hills.

A Marine assigned to H&S could, and frequently did, find himself stuck with his right hand raised over his eyebrow in salute as hundreds of lieutenants raced down the road hurrying to their next class or exercise. That night the same Marine, face and hands covered in black grease-paint, might find himself crawling on his belly until he crept to within two yards of a lieutenant assigned to guard duty, who had yet to learn how to use his peripheral vision to pierce the curtain of black in front of him, and whispering, "Lieutenant, you're dead; turn yourself in."

H&S Battalion was populated, as a result of those needs, with about one hundred cooks and stewards and two hundred Viet Nam veterans whose skills as killers and survivors had been refined in the crucible of jungle warfare—something the lieutenants could, for the moment, only imagine.

The Marine Corps is neither constituted nor designed as a subtle instrument of war. Its basic element is a fireteam, four men with rifles and the will to use them and the expectation they will see the men they kill. But while Marines are proud of their atavistic approach to war, they are never corporately, and seldom personally, suicidal. Within the confines of their mission and mentality, their tool kit is highly sophisticated. Among those tools, one of the most useful and unique is close air support.

To the Marine Corps, an airplane is a highly mobile platform for medium and large ordinance. To a second lieutenant fighting for real estate the same way a football team does—one yard at a time—the ability to call down strafing .50-caliber machine-gun fire or a sheet of white phosphorus immediately in front of his platoon is a very useful talent. But this technique involves high risks to the Marines in the air and on the ground, as well as the enemy. Flying a jet airplane low and slow enough to be effective against the enemy and without killing your own is a skill requiring at least as much courage and judgment as landing on the deck of a ship pitching and rolling on a stormy sea. And as for those on the ground, Marine riflemen swear there is nothing as deadly as a lieutenant with a map. A lieutenant who can't read one well enough to call out his coordinates exactly risks bringing that burning sheet of white phosphorus down on his own. Deadly indeed.

The dangers inherent in close air support, even in controlled conditions, are such that much of the technique is simulated during training. The aircraft used are propeller driven rather than jet propelled, T-34 Trainers being favored. This greatly reduces the risk of slow, low flight for the pilots. And to ensure against the risk of death and injury from misplaced aerial ordinance, the airplanes don't actually drop bombs. That effect is simulated by the explosion of a fifty-five gallon drum of motor oil.

Preparation for the exercise commences by digging holes in the ground deep enough to bury the oil drums. These are placed at points along the battle line where "enemy resistance" will be strongest. A single stick of dynamite, with blasting cap attached, is placed at the bottom of each hole. A pair of electric wires are attached to the cap and run out of the hole and strung across the terrain to a master board. The oil drum is then placed in the hole and covered over with dirt. Each master board, to which four to six pairs of wire are attached, is controlled by a demolition expert. He lies quietly in front of his board observing his charges and the sky above. When he sees the airplane diving toward one of them, he pulls a pair of wires off the master board and holds them over a battery. As the plane pulls up from its bombing run, he places the wires on the terminals of the battery, which sends an electric charge to the blasting cap, igniting the dynamite, which in turn explodes the oil, sending its covering dirt and a sheet of flame skyward. It gives the appearance to the advancing lieutenants that the aircraft has dropped a bomb just in front of them.

The Table of Organization for H&S Battalion called for ten demolition experts as part of its complement. This was because any given exercise might require as many as fifty such "bombs," and fifty bombs required eight to ten demolition experts to control them.

Demolition experts are unique men and unique Marines. They are men who are fascinated by charges and blasts, and compelled to, in an instant, destroy the work of other human beings that took days and months or even years to create. They enjoy the power that enables them, at the flick of a switch, to remove, as though it never existed, work representing the intellect, ingenuity, and labor of their fellow man. I do not mean to say there are no demolition experts in the United States Marine Corps who are not ordinary, level-headed souls whom circumstance directed to the work. But I am saying there are many who were the same young men who lit cherry bombs and flushed them down urinals just to see if it were true that you could blow one right off the wall. And when given the chance to indulge their nihilistic instinct in a socially sanctioned way, they took it with glee and without a second thought.

Guy Beaulieu, "Frenchy" to everyone in the battalion, was a demolitions expert. He was one of a handful of Canadians who thought to make up for the thousands of young Americans flocking to their country to avoid the draft by coming south to fight the American war. He had served two tours in Viet Nam, destroying all that was asked of him. Frenchy had a light heart and bright personality. His toothy smile and lilting *"Bon jour"* could bring a grin from the hardest of his companions. But despite his good work and demeanor, two tours in country had not brought him above the rank of lance corporal. His book was sprinkled with minor infractions and breaches of military protocol, and while none of them bore real malice they all represented what his high school guidance counselor no doubt called "low impulse control" and which a series of commanding officers had recorded as "ill-suited for leadership" and "lacking in military bearing."

Frenchy, like all the other demolition experts in the battalion, had labored all day yesterday preparing for today's exercise. The lieutenants were to have their first experience with close air support. The plan called for two companies of lieutenants to assault the H&S defenders through the denuded winter wood. The defenders would retreat in an orderly fashion up Iwo Jima Ridge. At the top of the ridge, the wood opened to a meadow of some hundred acres. Here the defenders would rapidly retreat around the edges of the meadow, leaving the assaulting lieutenants to find themselves with seven hundred yards of open ground before them. At that point their instructors would call in close air support. The "demo-guys" had buried fifty oil drums in the meadow, and, as the lieutenants slowly crossed the ground, air support dispatched from nearby MCAS Quantico would "drop bombs," opening a path before them.

The cold winter had frozen the Virginia ground to a foot deep and the demo guys had, despite the cold, found themselves stripped to their T-shirts and swinging mattocks to dig holes for the charges. But that had been yesterday.

This morning they'd been out here since 0400 hours, making final preparation for the dawn exercise. Wires had been run to the master boards under generator-powered floodlights. That had lasted until 0600. Since then, Frenchy and the others had been huddled in sleeping bags next to their boards. Despite double socks, field jacket, and a balaclava, Frenchy was cold. Marine Corps–issue cold-weather bag or no, the Goddamn ground was frozen, and lying on it was cold. Viet Nam may have been a leech and snake–infested swamp, but it was a warm leech and snake–infested swamp. Warm. Warm just like the broad ass on that BAM. She wasn't shit to look at, but she had an apartment in Dumfries. A Broad Assed Marine with an apartment was about as close to paradise as Frenchy was likely to come in the near future, and he'd left it at three A.M. for this. Her warm ass for this cold ground. *Merde! Fuckin' Marine Corps. Fuckin' lieutenants. Waste of time anyhow. They ain't gonna get this shit. Not one lieutenant in the Nam ever got this shit right. Platoon lose its sergeant and the lieutenant try to call in WP, odds are he's going to get the coordinates wrong. He'll fry his own Marines instead of Charlie. Bunch of dead Marines. Least the damn lieutenant be dead too. Where are those bastards? Cold! Fuckin' cold! Well at least it's light now. Sun's up soon.*

Frenchy was no more than ten yards inside the trees. Lying on his belly, he could see all the way up the meadow to the top of Iwo Jima Ridge. His five charges would be among the last to be exploded. The sergeant was somewhere off to his left about fifty yards, and one of the other guys was a like distance off to the right, but most of the unit was along the sides of the meadow. They'd blow the charges as the lieutenants assaulted down the hill.

Now he could make out the branches of the leafless tree canopy above him. It was black against the dark gray of the sky. He could no longer see stars. He heard a songbird behind him.

How do the damn birds survive in the winter? Too damn cold. Well they'll be here soon and we can get this happy horseshit done and go get warm.

A ray of sun blinded his left eye for a moment. He blinked and turned toward the east. *No warmth in it at all. But light. They'll be here soon.*

He sensed it before he heard it. At least if it was hearing, it was at a level he couldn't identify as such. And then he heard it and arched his neck to look up. High and in front of him. A steady low drone. *Plane's here. They'll be here already, calling her.*

Frenchy dropped his gaze to the ridgeline. *They're up there. Oh, yeah, there it is.* He couldn't see helmets but could make out the motion of a field radio antenna. *Fuckin' lieutenant doesn't even know what shows.*

Then the prop pitch on the T-34 got higher and louder. Frenchy could see it now, dropping down from the south, behind the lieutenants. The plane got big as it came down. Just above the ridge, maybe five hundred feet off the deck, the pilot pulled it back up and started to rise, the pitch of his engine deepening with the labor.

Because he knew where to look, Frenchy saw it before he heard it. Five hundred yards straight in front of him. That beautiful yellow flash only a cool flame makes. As he heard the roar, he saw the dirt flying up around the edges of the flash. Frenchy did not have words for the thought, but he smiled a wide appreciative and warm smile. He was no longer cold.

As he lay watching, the second plane in the flight dove into view, extended even lower than the first. As he pulled out of the dive and started back up, Frenchy's concentration was rewarded with another warming explosion—and then a third, as yet another plane followed.

After the third explosion the lieutenants appeared at the top of the hill and started down. The ballet of low, slow diving runs followed by yellow flashes and dirt eruptions, followed by advancing lieutenants, continued for ten minutes. Frenchy watched each blast with the rapt attention of a practitioner enamored of his craft. It was lovely. True, it was pretense with no destruction except dried meadow grasses, but it was as close as he'd come to the real thing save a third trip to Viet Nam.

With the lieutenants halfway across the meadow and the last explosion even closer, Frenchy pulled off his gloves and wrapped one wire of his most remote charge around the battery terminal. The silhouette of the T-34 became large as it dove toward his number-one charge. The pilot, warmed to his task, brought the plane to two hundred feet before he V-ed up sharply and pulled to the sky at full power. Frenchy lovingly laid the second wire against the other battery terminal and was instantly rewarded with a blast of his own.

He sighed. *Kind of like jacking off. Good, but not the real thing.*

The whine of a propeller and the black outline of the T-34 growing large punctured his reverie. Light pierced the bubble of plexiglas over the pilot and Frenchy could see the flyer's head and shoulders silhouetted in the cockpit. *I can actually see his eyes. He's focused on the mound over my number-two charge.*

Frenchy had one wire around the battery pole and lay staring straight into the flyer's face. It was almost upon him. *That's as low as he'll bring her.* And Frenchy touched the wire to the terminal. The plane flew into a rising curtain of flame, oil, and debris.

Explosions require three things: fuel, charge, and oxygen. Internal combustion engines require the same three. Frenchy's number-two charge and the T-34 each supplied its own fuel and charge, but they both depended on ambient oxygen. Given the proximity of the two, it was the same oxygen for which they competed. The blast, being the more voracious, won, and the airplane engine failed to fire.

An airplane doesn't require an engine to fly. It requires air speed. So long as the plane moves fast enough, the vacuum above the wing will keep it flying. But slow the air speed sufficiently and the airplane will stall. And a stalled airplane falls from the sky.

The pilot of the T-34 knew all of this when his engine failed two hundred feet above the ground. He knew he was flying, engine or no, but flying straight toward his death. He also knew that to pull up, to turn away from death, without an engine to provide pull, would almost instantly reduce his air speed below stall speed and he would fall from the sky. He must have known all of this with an instinct beyond cognition, because what he did, flying straight toward the ground and completely blinded by oil on his windshield, was nothing. He let the airplane fly. It flew out of the moment of time and space deprived of oxygen and found more. The T-34 coughed twice and fired again. Only then did the pilot pull away from violent death. Less than fifty feet from the ground he rose up as sharply as the plane would allow, cleared the trees at meadow's edge by an imperceptible margin and flew, away.

All explosions stopped, but the lieutenants came on. Who would expect the dumb bastards to understand?

"Jesus Christ, Frenchy, what did you do that for?"

Frenchy stared up at his Sergeant, his expression beatific and remote.

"Was it an accident?"

Frenchy's eyes slowly came into focus and then a wry grin formed at the corners of his mouth.

"God damn it, Frenchy. You asshole! You could have killed him."

Brush snapped beside them as another demo guy rushed up.

"What the hell happened, Sarge?" the newcomer demanded.

The Sergeant's eyes gave way to surprise. "Kendrick, what the hell are you doing here?"

"Thought I'd see what you demo guys do out here. I came out with your coffee at 0400."

"Picked the wrong time, College Boy." The Sergeant turned to Frenchy and kicked at his bag. "God damn it, get up."

"*Oww!*"

"Get the fuck up. What a mess."

"So what are you gonna do, Sarge?"

The Sergeant ignored him and addressed Frenchy, who was now scrambling to get his legs free of the sleeping bag. "God damn you."

"Sarge, we gonna do anything? Those lieutenants gonna be here in about two minutes."

"Listen shithead, the lieutenants are the least of our problems. Criminal Investigation Division is going to be here about ten minutes after that flyboy calls in for instructions for an instrument approach—which is about now."

Frenchy looked concerned for the first time. "El Cid? Jesus!"

"Oh, fuck you, Frenchy. What the hell did you think was gonna happen when you decided to down a fuckin' fighter with friendly fire?"

"I didn't—"

"Oh, shut the fuck up. I gotta think. I gotta think." The Sergeant kicked Frenchy's master board and it bounced off a nearby hickory, wires flying.

"Sarge, would that work?" Kendrick asked.

"What the fuck you talking about?"

"Scramble all the wires."

The Sergeant gasped. "Shit. That's it! Frenchy, get your board." He nodded at Kendrick. "You too. Both of you meet me out there." He pointed to the meadow and the advancing lieutenants. "Now move." And the Sergeant disappeared back into the wood from where he'd come.

Within minutes the three Marines were standing in the middle of the meadow being passed by assaulting lieutenants in full combat gear who seemed entirely uncertain what to make of them. The Sergeant made huge beckoning motions toward the Marine demolitions experts positioned around the sides of the meadow. Soon they were all gathered.

"Okay, you all saw it. If I don't miss my guess El Cid's gonna be here in minutes and I suspect the General's right behind them. We cover Frenchy's ass or he's dead meat."

"Shit, I didn't do—"

"Frenchy, I thought I told you to shut up."

Frenchy looked down at his boots.

"Agreed?" The Sergeant looked around the group and, in turn, made eye contact with each Marine.

Each met his eyes.

"Okay, Frenchy, give me a wire from your number-two charge, and here, take one of mine. One of you swap one of your wires for the other wire from Frenchy's number-two charge. And all of you trade with each other. Everything you've got. Within two minutes, I want the charge wires in this meadow to look like a worm farm. Once you're done, race around the lieutenants back to our vehicle and retreat before the advancing lieutenants as planned. "And all of you. The wires gonna be the easy part. El Cid is gonna make it very hot on every one of us." He nodded at Frenchy. "Asshole here is a lot of trouble, but he's ours. This ain't gonna be easy, but if we stick together we'll make it.

"*Semper Fi.*"

It wasn't easy, and they did make it.

Courts Martial General

Friday March 29, 1968

"KENDRICK, YOU GOT my leave papers?"

Jack finished typing the line, threw the carriage, and was rewarded with a satisfying *ding* before he looked up to see Corporal Buck's smile flooding down upon him. Buck was one of those Negroes with skin so dark it glowed in an almost iridescent way. The black skin in contrast to the white teeth gave the man's smile a compelling quality that wouldn't allow it to be taken for granted—seen but not noticed like the ubiquitous drab cream color of the walls. But the effect of Buck's smile was not just an accident of angstrom-rays, Jack had long since decided. Buck was a man who carried with him a sense that the world was good and would treat him well, and he projected that beneficent reality before him.

"What's up, Bud?" Jack couldn't help but smile back at the

handsome dark face with hair so closely buzzed that the ears extended like black half hearts on either side of his head.

"Why you call me that, Kendrick? You know it's not my name."

"Just a beach thing, Corporal Buck. Sorry."

They looked silently at one another for a moment. Jack had not a clue what Buck was thinking but enjoyed the small discomfiture his West Coast slang caused this son of the Mississippi Delta.

Buck broke the silence. "Leave. Papers. You got 'em for me?"

"Oh, yeah. I think so. Scotty, did the Captain sign Buck's leave papers?" Kendrick asked the Marine sitting at the desk beside the C.O.'s door.

Without looking up, Sergeant Scott answered, "Said he would leave them on his desk. Take a look."

"I'll get them." Jack pushed back his wooden chair and listened to the scraping sound the brass brads in the bottoms of the legs made as they were dragged across the linoleum tile. Four steps led him past Scotty's desk and to the company commander's open door.

A half-inch–thick brown manila folder with a neatly typed label, "Buck, William / Corporal," pasted to its three-cut tab lay squarely centered on the Captain's desk blotter. Without picking it up, Kendrick opened the folder. The top document was a crisp sheet of paper labeled:

LEAVE ORDERS
CORPORAL WILLIAM BUCK
03/30/68–04/05/68

It was signed at the bottom in a bold scrawl: Captain Benjamin Posee USMC(R)

Kendrick pulled out the orders, closed the file, turned, and departed. Buck stood where Jack had left him, freshly pressed utilities neatly bloused over boots that shone like they were ready for inspection. He held his cover in both hands slowly turning its sharply pressed and starched edges through his fingers.

Extending the orders toward him, Jack asked, "Where you off to, Bud?"

Seeing the scowl darken Buck's normally beaming countenance, Jack corrected, "Err. Corporal Buck?"

Buck's expression lightened. "Going home, Kendrick."

"Home?"

"Gonna get me some o' Momma's home cookin'."

"Big family?"

"Naw. Just me and Momma. I'm all she's got now. Gotta look out for her."

"She's lucky to have you. Not everyone around here spends leave looking out for his mother."

"More in it than that. I gotta get work."

"Work?"

Buck's teeth flashed pearlized warmth across the desk. "Short-timer's calendar down to thirty-two days. April 30 this Marine is promoted to civilian."

"God, I envy you. I've still got 351."

"But who's counting?"

Both Marines laughed.

"What you gonna do?"

"What the Marine Corps taught me, Kendrick."

Kendrick said nothing, knowing Buck would continue.

"I'm gonna cook. Or if I get lucky, ramrod a bunch of other cooks." Buck unbuttoned the flap of the breast pocket of his blouse and extracted a neatly trimmed newspaper clipping. "Momma mailed it last week. Hojo's on I-40 is lookin' for a supervisor of the night crew. I'm a non-commissioned officer who runs a kitchen that feeds 1,500 per meal. Think I'm qualified?"

"Long as they don't eat your mashed potatoes."

"At ease, Lance Corporal." The mock frown remained on Buck's face only momentarily. "Well, I gotta run. Bus outta' Dumfries in an hour."

Kendrick extended his hand and Buck took it in his own firm, strong grip. "Good huntin', Bud...err, Corporal Buck."

"See ya a week from Saturday." Buck turned and left.

Jack could hear the steady cadence of his heels echoing off the linoleum as Buck made his solo departure down the passageway. "At least our Captain did what he promised and didn't make Buck miss his bus."

"Humph" was all he got out of Scott.

"YOU give Buck his leave orders?"

Kendrick looked up into the stern, round face of Captain Benjamin Posee staring down harshly. "Yes, Sir."

"Here." The Captain extended Buck's book toward him. "Put this away."

Kendrick accepted the offered folder. "Yes, Sir."

The Captain dropped his hand to his side, pointed the toe of his right shoe into the linoleum behind him, turned smartly to his right, and stared down at Sergeant Scott. "Sergeant, we're getting flabby."

"Sir?" the sergeant looked up with a quizzical expression that caused his brow to furrow.

"This company is about to take off some winter fat."

Scott just stared back up from his chair.

"Before weekend liberty, type up an order. Starting next week, the entire company, except morning watch, is going to run. Assembly at 0700 in fatigues, boots, and soft-covers. Tuesdays and Thursdays. I'll sign it. You get it posted Monday."

"Yes, Sir."

"And Scott, you personally see Sergeant Townsend gets the word. I don't want any Goddamn confusion with that crew of his."

"Yes, Sir."

The Captain turned and departed.

"Have a good weekend, Sir." Scott's voice followed the Captain out the door and down the hall.

"Son of a bitch," Jack muttered under his breath.

"Don't want to run at 0700, Jack?"

"Scotty, I'll run any time and beat your skinny ass—his too." Jack jerked his thumb toward the still open door.

"Then why the whining?"

"'Cause Captain tough-guy there is gonna show up in soft shoes and prove how bad he is by testing himself against Marines running in boots."

"Yeah, maybe he can use that white German Shepherd to pull him, too."

Both men laughed.

"You're right about our OCS motor pool officer being a wannabe, but one part you're wrong about, Jack."

"What's that?" It was Kendrick's turn to look quizzical.

"All you'll be seeing of my skinny ass at the finish line is the back of it.

Tuesday April 2, 1968

BY 0700 the sun had given enough warmth to take some spring chill out of the air. It also illuminated the light green buds covering every branch of every tree in the Northern Virginia woods. Songbirds serenaded the sixty-five Marines all dressed in olive-drab fatigues and gathered in the far corner of the four-acre parade ground.

"I've got a buck says the asshole's gonna bring that sled dog to pull 'im."

The laugh it drew held no warmth.

As though on cue the Captain appeared across the grinder. At this distance, none of them would have recognized him were it not for the snow-white dog heeled at his side.

"Form it up, assholes. Column of fours," Sergeant Townsend barked at the loosely assembled company. "Dress the line. Let's look preddy for the man."

The Marines fell in four abreast. Each man turned to the Marine on his right to make certain he was in line. Here and there, a right arm came up to shoulder height to check spacing.

When it was done, Townsend barked, "By the left flank."

They froze in anticipation.

"Huh," Townsend barked again, and each man took one stride forward on his right foot, pivoted to his left on the balls of both feet, closed his left foot to his right, and froze. The company now presented a line sixteen long and four deep attentively awaiting their approaching Captain.

"Good morning, Sergeant Townsend. Is the company present and accounted for?"

As the Captain stopped to address the Sergeant his dog dropped his hindquarters and sat, tongue lolling out, chromed choke chain gleaming and teeth showing.

"Yes, Sir."

Standing in the second row, Jack observed Captain Posee's black, high-top Converses.

"All right, men, here's the drill. We'll take a lap around the grinder at double time. After one lap, I'll lead us off into the woods. Still at double time, we'll proceed to the rifle range and back. Somewhere before we get back, I'll release you to race back here." He paused momentarily. "Hansen, you here?" His eyes searched the company.

"Here, Sir," one of the cooks in the rear drawled.

"Front and center, Hansen."

The Marine stepped through the ranks and presented himself at attention before the officer.

"Rommel here likes you. Someone needs to hold him while we run. Care to volunteer?"

"Yes, Sir."

The Captain handed him the leash and turned to Townsend. "Lead them out, Sergeant."

Townsend barked, "Double time. March."

Sixty-five Marines in formation jogged around the grinder and then down the road. Twenty minutes later they reached the rifle range, circled around, and headed back.

"Jack, you gonna wimp out or you gonna race me in when he releases us?" Scotty panted lightly as they trotted along three rows behind the Captain and Townsend.

"Be damned if that pudgy prick is gonna get any additional sweat out of me," Jack responded.

"It's gonna do that or watch him gloat. Either way the gutless bastard wins."

"Prick." Jack wasn't sure who he meant.

With about a mile to go, the Captain's voice shouted back over the company, "I want a footrace now. Formation is broken. Let's go." And he accelerated away from the group.

Most of the group maintained pace and wouldn't be baited into working any harder than they had too. About half a dozen took off after the Captain in an open race to the finish.

"Jack."

He looked over at a smiling Scott.

"Gloats worse. Let's go, hoss." And Scotty picked up the pace and moved forward through the line.

"God damn it," Jack muttered. He lowered his head and took off after the streaking Scott.

He dragged the Captain down with a quarter of a mile to go. Scott was harder to catch, but Jack sped past him as they passed Hansen still holding tightly onto Rommel's leash.

Pudgy little truck driver, Jack thought as he coasted to a stop, leaning over with his hands on his knees to catch his breath. *Fucking poser.*

Friday April 5, 1968

THE footfalls coming down the hall toward him were rapid, something just short of a run.

"Kendrick, is the skipper in yet?"

Sergeant Townsend's light complexion was positively

florid. *He must have run up the hill and slowed to force himself into a walk once he reached the building,* Jack thought.

"It's important."

"Good morning, Sergeant Townsend."

Both Marines turned to see the fire-plug figure of Captain Posee filling the inner office door.

Townsend turned to face the Captain and braced to attention. "You've heard, Sir?"

"Heard what?"

"That nigger minister—"

"Sergeant Townsend, what did you just say?"

"Sorry, Sir. Let me rephrase that. Did the Captain hear that the Negro minister—Dr. King—was killed? Shot, Sir. In the head, I believe."

"I heard that in the car on the way in. Why rush up here, Townsend?"

Jack watched Townsend's posture become even more rigid as he straightened to full height.

"Sir, permission to speak freely?" The Sergeant stared at a spot above the Captain's head.

"Granted."

"Sir, this is a cooks' company." He continued to stare at the spot.

Captain Posee looked intently toward the Sergeant but did not speak.

"Half the Marines here are...Negroes, Sir."

"Your point being, Sergeant?"

"Sir, it was on the news at the NCO Club last night. There was grumbling among the Negro NCOs. It was still going on this morning at chow."

"At ease, Sergeant."

Townsend's posture relaxed a bit as he snapped his feet to shoulder width and pulled both hands into the small of his back.

The Captain continued. "What sort of grumbling, Sergeant?"

The Sergeant now looked at the Captain and addressed him directly. "They whined about justice in the South. Oppression. You know, Sir, the usual nigger stuff."

"Townsend, that's enough. You will not use that word here." After a pause he asked, "Any specific threats, Sergeant, from any specific Marines?"

"No, Sir."

The Captain stood for a moment with an unfixed gaze. His eyes suddenly came back into focus on Townsend. "That will be all, Sergeant." He then spun around with a speed that belied his girth and disappeared back into his office, closing the door behind him.

Jack sat looking up at the dismissed sergeant.

"What the hell are you staring at, Marine?"

Sergeant Townsend had found a new object of displeasure.

"Just watching your discussion with the Captain, Sergeant."

"When's Buck due back?"

"O eight hundred, tomorrow."

"We'll see." The Sergeant's lips formed a tight, malevolent grin, and he left.

Jack turned to look at his office mate. "What the hell was that about?"

"It would appear that Sergeant Townsend doesn't like Negroes. Even Negro Marines."

"I got that, Scotty. But the part about the NCO Club. What was he talking about?"

"You, young Lance Corporal, being a commuter, sometimes miss the joys of base life."

"So what did I miss last night?" Jack asked.

"You heard about Martin Luther King, Jr.?"

"The assassination was all over the radio as I drove back to D.C. last night."

"Radio on that old truck of yours still works, huh?"

"It's the floorboards the Marine Corps let rust out before they surveyed it, not the radio," Jack answered. "So what happened at the Club?"

"It wasn't just the Club, Jack. It was all over the battalion compound. Black Marines were mad. Most of us white guys didn't get it. It'll blow over."

Jack nodded and looked down at his in-box. When he looked back up Scott was already at work.

"Scotty?"

The thin patrician face across from him looked back up.

"One more thing, Scotty. What did Townsend mean about Buck?"

Scott's piercing blue eyes stared unblinking. "Reverend King was killed in Memphis."

"Yeah?" Jack nodded blankly.

"Buck's home."

JACK answered the phone. "Maintenance Support Company. Lance Corporal Kendrick, speaking."

"Kendrick, the Skipper in?"

"Buck? How you doing, Bud?"

"No good, Kendrick."

"What's wrong?"

"What's wrong? You don't get no news at all? Guys in the street all over Memphis. Riots and some fires. It's bad here."

"When's your bus back?"

"Five o'clock tonight."

"Well hop on that dog and get out of there."

"Can't do that, Kendrick."

"Why not?"

"Momma, Kendrick. I can't leave her here alone. People gettin' hurt round here, and it's gonna get worse."

"Hold on. I'll give you to Captain Posee. How much leave you got left?"

"Two days, Kendrick. That's it 'til I'm out."

"Okay, Buck, I'll put you on the horn with the Captain. And, Buck…"

"Yeah?"

"You get the job?"

"Night cook supervisor. Three twenty-five an hour. Starting May seventh."

"Way to go, Bud."

"Thanks, Kendrick."

Scott sat straight up, looking, but said nothing.

Kendrick hit the hold button, pushed back from his chair, and walked across the small outer office to the Captain's door. He positioned himself in the middle of the open space and rapped twice, sharply on the frame.

"Come," the tenor boomed.

Kendrick took one step in and turned to the right, facing the Captain's desk. The room was Spartan with a desk toward the rear and the Captain sitting in a government-issue swivel chair behind it. He was flanked by two flag stands. One held the US flag, the other that of the USMC. In the corner near a side door, Rommel lay curled on a cedar pad. The dog and the Captain both looked quizzically.

"Kendrick."

"Corporal Buck on the phone for you, Sir."

"What's he want?"

"He's in Memphis, Sir. With his mother. Says the place is burning down."

"Put him through, Kendrick."

Kendrick stepped back into the outer office, reached across his desk, hit the button on his phone which would transfer the held call to the Captain. He then wheeled to face the bank of steel file cabinets that lined one wall, opened the drawer marked "CA—DO", and pulled the folio labeled "Buck, William / Corporal." Kendrick swiftly thumbed through the pages until he came to one labeled "Leave Computation." Buck was right. Only two days leave remaining before discharge. Kendrick held the folio open to the page and walked slowly back toward the Captain's door, awaiting the call he knew would come.

"Kendrick."

He stepped through the door, turned right and braced.

"Sir."

"That Buck's book?"

"Yes, Sir."

"Let's have it."

Kendrick took two steps to the desk and presented the demanded folio to the Captain's extended hand.

The Captain set the folio before him, scanned the page quickly, and then picked up the receiver lying on his desk. "Buck, your leave is extended for two days. You're due here at 0800 Monday. And, Buck, if you're late, you're AWOL." He cradled the receiver, folded the folio and, without looking up, extended it back to Kendrick. "Type up the appropriate order for my signature and bring Buck's book current before you leave for the day."

"Sir." Kendrick accepted the folio and departed.

"Captain extend his leave?" Scott asked.

Jack nodded as he rolled the form into the carriage of his typewriter.

"How long did he give him?" Scott continued.

"No more than he's earned."

"That's the best he could do?" Scott allowed.

"That's the best he could do."

Jack finished typing the order extending Buck's leave, got the Captain's signature; two-hole punched the form, and put it in Buck's book.

"What's up this weekend, Jack? Gonna chase hippie chicks?"

"You mean after I replumb the toilet in that basement hovel my Marine Corps housing allotment gets me?"

"Well, buddy, if you didn't insist on living in D.C. instead of on base—"

Jack cut him off. "I know. I could replumb toilets in some barracks at MCB Quantico."

Scott chuckled and smiled.

"But you're right about the other part, Scotty."

"How's that?"

"Nothing big-breasted hippy chicks with no bras and peasant blouses would rather do than throw themselves at guys with white-sidewall haircuts. We're real popular out there." Jack rolled his eyes.

Saturday April 6, 1968

THE reflection of the crisp white of the monolith extended toward him with the spire at the top ending less than fifty feet from his crossed legs. He was tempted to dangle his bare feet in the water, but the ripples would have distorted the illusion. And he liked the illusion. It was one of his favorite sites in all of Washington. When no breeze upset the water's surface and the reflection of Washington's monument extended the entire length of the pool, sitting here with Lincoln at his back and the legacy of Washington pointed straight toward him filled him with a sense of purpose. Made him feel he wasn't wrong about all this.

Barefoot and dressed in faded jeans and a white T-shirt, he almost fit. And he suspected the others here even sought the same things he did. Some atavistic impulse led them all to bathe in the first warm sun of the year—just to soak in the warmth and the light and know the harsh reality of winter was no longer with them. They had outlived it one more time. But they could do that on any commons, green, or park. Those who came here wanted that and something more. Here, they, like Jack, wished to be reassured that they also enjoyed the goodwill of the Founders. They wanted to know that their position was not just theirs but, while the circumstances were new, their critical thinking regarding the social compact and their obligation to their fellows and their government came from a long and democratic intellectual thread that was spun, in part, by the champions who were honored here.

He could tell from the dress and manner of most of the others here (the long and flowing hair, the garlands of flowers and beads, the sandals, bell-bottoms, and headbands) that they connected those dots very differently from him and drew very different conclusions. He suspected their conclusions were cowardly and self-serving. He also knew that they suspected his were mindlessly conforming and shaped by a testosterone-driven brutality.

"Hey, bro, if I'm not mistaken that's a baby killer sitting by the edge of the pool."

Jack knew without looking up that his moment of quiet reflection had ended. Without rising or even uncrossing his legs he turned to look across the grass behind him. There were six of them. Four were young men about his age, each with long stringy hair and the best attempts at beards they could offer. The two women were about the same age as the men and equally unkempt. It was a style that on women gave a sense of wildness and lack of constraint, but on men just looked scruffy. The tallest of the young men faced him squarely, feet apart and hands on his hips. The others stood slightly behind him.

"I'll let that go...once."

Jack noted the hems of the tall one's bell-bottoms fluttered as he shifted his weight deciding whether to advance or retreat. As Jack watched, one of the girls put a hand on the man's forearm and pulled him backward.

"Don't, Shaggy. No need for that."

She was barefoot, and as she stepped in front of Shaggy her denim skirt undulated with her stride. Her white linen peasant blouse was pulled down off her shoulders. Her dark hair flowed loose except where the strands braided up from the nape of her neck held it in place across the crown of her head. The brown eyes that held his were soft with tranquility or drugs. He couldn't tell which.

She quietly covered the three paces that separated them, took a crocus from the braid across her crown, leaned down and placed it in his hand.

No bra.

"You're in the Army, aren't you?" Her voice was soft like her eyes but not drugged.

"Marine Corps," Jack answered and could not contain the impulse to gaze down the draped bodice at her rounded dangling breasts.

Brown nipples.

He looked back up at the unblinking eyes no more than two feet above.

"Why do you do it?" she asked.

Jack could not let go of the eyes, but he did let go of the anger.

"Duty."

"Duty!" It was a shriek from Shaggy. "Duty to who? The military industrial complex?"

Jack spun around in the grass, rose from his lotus seat in a single motion, and covered the distance between them in two strides.

"Shaggy. Is that your name?"

Jack stood ramrod straight looking up slightly into the hostile eyes.

Shaggy nodded.

"Ever read Plato, Shaggy?"

The eyes became uncertain and then hateful.

"Plato didn't know shit about western imperialism, dude."

"You're wrong, Shaggy. He knew a great deal about imperialism, but that's not the point."

"And what is the point, jarhead?"

Shaggy had moved close now, almost towering above. The other three men moved to encircle him.

"Duty, Shaggy, duty. That's the point. Socrates had it pretty clear. Not one man in a hundred can live alone outside the polis. So we owe the polis our life, and if it calls on us we only have two choices."

"And one's to become a baby killer?"

Jack's opened hand shot out and closed instantly on Shaggy's windpipe, fingers on one side, thumb on the other—digging in. Jack pressed forward and up as hard as he could forcing the tall man up onto his toes.

Shaggy gasped his mouth open, his eyes wide.

"I told you I'd let that go once, asshole," Jack hissed.

"Jesus, dude. You'll kill him."

"Stop!"

"Stop!"

Jack threw Shaggy away from him as he let go. The tall man went straight over backwards, grabbing at his throat and hacking. His friends all fell back from Jack in genuine fear and revulsion.

"Get him out of here. Now," Jack ordered.

Jack watched as they scrambled to get their friend up and away from his demon. He sat back down at the edge of the pool to wait for the adrenalin to wash away.

Jack stared again at the water. Washington continued to point straight at him. He turned and looked behind him at the tall old wrestler with the gaunt and bearded face staring benevolently down at him.

He felt her presence before he heard her. It was the same soft voice.

"What were the two choices he offered?"

Jack turned toward the voice. She was sitting in the same cross-legged posture he was in, slightly behind him and to his left.

He took all of her in before he spoke. Skirt spread out full around her, hands folded in her lap holding another crocus.

"Socrates?"

"Yes."

He thought long before he answered. "You know anything about plumbing?"

She smiled at him, shy, almost coquettish. "I know something about joints."

Monday April 8, 1968

"MAINTENANCE Support Company. Lance Corporal Kendrick speaking."

"Kendrick, the Skipper in?"

"Buck, tell me you're calling from the bus station in Dumfries, and you need a ride."

"I'm calling from Momma's, Kendrick."

"Bud, you're AWOL in thirty minutes. Absent Without Leave. You know, the one where the USMC says nasty things about you and does nasty things to you."

"Kendrick, I ain't Superman, and I ain't gonna get from

Memphis, Tennessee to Quantico, Virginia in no thirty minutes. Now's the Skip in or not?"

Kendrick exhaled and sat silently with the receiver in his ear.

"Kendrick?"

"Yeah, I'm here. Look, Buck, I'll get him, but give me your mom's number just in case."

Buck did, and Jack wrote it down before putting the call on hold and crossing the room to the Captain's office door, where he knocked smartly.

"Come."

"Sir. Corporal Buck is on the horn for you, Sir."

"What's he want, Kendrick?"

"He's still in Memphis, Sir. Line one."

The Captain picked up the phone and punched the button. "Buck." The Captain said no more and listened, the receiver jammed tightly to his ear, his face a scowl.

"Corporal, you are Absent Without Leave. I appreciate that your motives are admirable, but you should have thought of that before you used up all your time. I have no more to give you. Your violation starts at 0800 and will continue until you turn yourself in. Report to my office the instant you get back on base."

And he hung up.

Only then did the Captain seem to realize that Kendrick was still in his office.

"What do you want?"

Kendrick looked intently at his commanding officer. "Sir, the radio reported there are still riots and fires in Memphis."

"What's that got to do with me, Kendrick?"

"Sir, may I ask you a question?"

The response was silence.

"What would you do, Sir? Would you leave her there? Alone?"

"That will be all, Lance Corporal."

The two men's eyes held for a moment. Without averting his gaze, Kendrick came to attention, placed the toe of his boot on the floor behind him, spun, and departed.

THE Staff Sergeant paced. Six paces across the office, about face, six paces back. Repeat. The mandarin collar chafed. He liked recruiting duty. He liked wearing dress blues—looked good in them and he knew it. The girls on Beale Street knew it too. Thursday one even whistled as he walked home. He also liked helping young men find a way, a place, home. But mostly he liked not being shot at. One tour was enough. Here it was safe. At least it had been until Friday.

Christ, he'd seen less confusion and fire in a burning "vil" than he'd seen in Memphis on Friday night.

Fucking cowardly bastard. Shot Dr. King like that—in ambush. Prick. Fucking prick. No wonder they're pissed. But what a bunch of fools. Fools. Pissed at Whitey so we burned down our own damned houses. Fools.

He'd been glad for this duty. Glad to come home an example, a Marine. Now he wasn't so sure. At least on base there was order. Sure, a few guys were bigots, and more than a handful of the ninety-day wonders were pricks, but mostly The Corps was family. He had place.

But if not here, where? Pendleton. then back to WestPac. Back to "the Nam."

Christ, I hope not.

He stopped pacing when he saw him outside the glass. Head down, hands in pockets, and coming quickly. Black. Maybe twenty-two. Thin. Muscular chest obvious beneath the unzipped Eisenhower jacket as he came across the street mid-block. Straight for the door.

A recruit? Riots make up his mind to get out?

The door opened. The man walked in, shut it, and braced.

Not a recruit. Not with that haircut and posture.

Neither man spoke. They looked at each other in open assessment. Buck spoke first.

"Staff Sergeant, I'm AWOL."

KENDRICK studied the school clock on the wall. Almost seventeen hundred. Captain was gone. Scotty was gone. Three minutes, he'd be gone.

His loins ached. He'd tried to be very quiet as he dressed and left this morning. Didn't want to spoil the dream. His last look back as he closed the door had shown him the curve of her hip, leg extended from under the covers, languid in the pre-dawn dim.

God, I hope she's still there.

The ringing telephone dissolved the fantasy.

"Maintenance Support—"

"Kendrick, Skipper in?"

"No, and he probably wouldn't speak to you if he were. Where are you?"

"I turned myself in."

"You what? Where?"

"USMC recruiter in Memphis."

"Why?" Kendrick insisted. "You need to get your ass back here."

"For a college boy, you ain't so smart, Kendrick. Or maybe just ignorant. I ain't AWOL no more, Kendrick. Stopped at 1500, soon as I turned myself in. So I'm only AWOL for seven hours. Maybe Skip won't have to do much more than chew my ass to the bone and work me twenty-four hours a day for the next twenty-two days."

Kendrick could feel the corners of his mouth pull up—way up. "N.J.P. Good get, Bud. No court, just Non-Judicial Punishment. Now what?"

"I got orders to return to my duty station—that would be you—and a ticket on the gray dog at twenty hundred hours. I'll be back by noon tomorrow. Noon. Kendrick, you tell Skip. You hear?"

"I'll tell 'im. Now you tell me, how's your mom?"

"Quiet as a church on Monday morning here. Police everywhere, but no fires and no gunshots. She's shook, but the house is intact. She'll be okay. See ya, College Boy."

Tuesday April 9, 1968
JACK stared fixedly into space at nothing, eyes focused somewhere between the row of manuals stacked across the front of his desk and in front of the metal file cabinets that lined the wall. His thoughts, if they existed at all, were equally out of focus. He became aware of a noise, a hum. The low-voltage hum of a very small electric motor. He resisted the pull of consciousness, but the sound of the motor, once recognized, drew him back.

He was thinking again—of time. *Time. God damn time.*

Buck wasn't here yet, and it was almost time. Jack looked up at the clock—big, round, with twelve distinct block numbers, each in its defined place and all surrounded by a solid black metal band. The short arm and the long dancing slowly together, one lying on top of the other, almost straight up. The longer and thinner hand dancing also, but to a much faster tune, racing from straight down to join its mates in their common salute to the meridian.

Jack shifted his eyes to the open space of the door. If he stared hard enough could he make Buck appear? No, the sound must precede him—boots on linoleum. All was quiet, no boots coming, not in time. All quiet but the low-voltage hum. Jack looked back up. One more tick. There, all three hands appeared in the elegant symmetry of straight up.

Tick. It was past noon.

"Damn."

Scotty's voice sounded more like a prayer than a curse.

"He'll be here, Scotty. Bus was due at Dumfries at eleven-fifteen. He'll be here."

"No he won't, Jack. Not in time."

"Sergeant Scott."

It was a command for presence.

Scotty's expression was all resignation. He rose and stepped around his desk and into the doorframe that defined the passage from their outer office to the Captain's. He did not enter, but stood on the threshold, his backside to Jack.

"Sir," he barked.

Captain Posee's voice was clear, almost crisp, across his office to Scott and then through the door and around the corner to Jack.

"Has Corporal Buck presented himself as ordered?"

"No, Sir. He has not."

"And you were clear on the call from the recruiter in Memphis. His orders were for arrival here by twelve hundred hours, Eastern Standard Time?"

"That is what the recruiter said, Sir."

"Call the MPs, Sergeant. Tell them Buck has missed a movement in defiance of orders and is to be arrested when sighted."

"Sir." Jack heard himself speak before he knew he would. He spoke loudly to project into the Captain's office and was up and across the floor and wedged into the doorframe beside Scott before he received a response.

"Sir, the bus could be late; he may be waiting for a cab; he may—"

"That will be all, Lance Corporal!"

"Sir, please at least let me check, Sir. If he got on that bus but the bus failed would he be in defiance, Sir?"

Captain Posee glared from the chair behind his desk, but didn't rise and didn't speak. Jack took it for permission.

"Sir," Jack spoke very softly now, trying intentionally to remove all emotion. "Sir, before we contact the MPs, at least grant me permission to call his mother and see if he got on the bus."

"We have her number?"

"I have it, Sir."

Captain Posee's glare softened. "Granted."

Jack tried to squeeze back past Sergeant Scott to the outer office. Captain Posee stopped him.

"Use mine." He pointed to the phone on his desk.

Jack gulped. "Sir, his number's on my desk."

"Get it and return."

Jack remained where he was, squeezed in next to Scott.

"Now!"

The command catapulted Jack to his desk. By the time he returned, Scott had vacated the door and was standing at parade rest just inside the Captain's office. Jack stepped in as Captain Posee picked up his phone, receiver still in place, turned it around and set it on the front edge of his desk.

The receiver was warm in Jack's palm as he picked it up. It felt clammy as well. Jack couldn't tell if the moisture was his or that of his commanding officer. He turned the dial slowly. It rang. Four times. Then five.

"Buck here."

Jack stammered and then looked directly at the Captain as he spoke.

"Corporal Buck?"

In the three seconds of stillness Jack's heart beat ten times.

"Kendrick, is that you?"

"Yeah, Buck, it's me. Buck, why aren't you here?"

"Tell you what, College Boy, you hold the phone for a minute. I'm gonna walk to the front door, open it, and hold the phone out and you tell me what you hear."

Jack could hear the footfalls over the line, then a click and the groan of a hinge in need of oil—then faintly a distant wail, then another over it—closer, and then soft popping noises.

"You hear it Kendrick?"

"Sirens and what sounds like seven point six two millimeter rounds going off."

Buck snorted. "Not a military range here. Thirty caliber is probably more like it. But you hear it, Kendrick?"

"Yeah, Buck, I hear it."

Jack looked at the commanding officer and extended the phone. The Captain didn't raise either hand from his desk. Jack continued to hold the receiver toward him. Slowly, and without losing eye contact, the Captain shook his head.

Jack put the phone back to his ear. "You keep her safe, Bud. We'll see you when you get here."

THE old lady seemed frail compared to the muscular young man whose arm she clutched tightly. She pulled him so close that they touched from hip to shoulder as they walked slowly. The crowd flooded around them on both sides, then slowed and came back together to form a single irregular line at the edge of the platform.

When they arrived at the back of the line, he pulled his arm from her grasp and put it around her shoulders and pulled her into him. Her gray unkempt hair spread across the chest of the olive-drab wool uniform her face had disappeared into. He enfolded the little woman into his long arms and held her. He stood with his back straight but with his head buried in her gray hair. She was completely still but for the spasmodic rise and fall of her shoulders.

The bus driver rested his hand on the metal crank, keeping the door open. "Marine, we gotta go. We were due to depart at ten P.M. We're already late."

He turned the small face up, held it in both hands, and kissed her forehead, then turned and stepped into the dark opening and up the steps. He made his way down the aisle and grabbed at the overhead rack as the air brakes hissed and the Greyhound lurched forward. He sat and stared out the window at the ever-diminishing figure of the sobbing woman at the edge of the platform.

Wednesday April 10, 1968

THE footfalls were regular but slow, almost leisurely, on the linoleum tile. Kendrick heard and knew. He looked at the school clock on the wall. Yesterday's clock. The little hand and the big lay one on top of the other and straight up. The red second hand racing up to join them.

He's right on time a day late, Kendrick thought.

Scott knew too. His gaze, along with Jack's, was fixed on the office door. The sound arrived and the door was filled with Buck. He smiled slowly down at Kendrick—no teeth, but a smile all the same.

"Corporal William Buck reporting as ordered."

Kendrick forced a wan smile. "I'll tell the Captain. Why don't you have a seat?" Kendrick nodded in the direction of the single steel chair just inside the door and in front of his desk.

Without looking to see if Buck accepted his offer, he rose and stepped to the Captain's open door. Standing squarely in the center of the opening, Kendrick rapped sharply on the frame.

"Come."

Stepping inside, Kendrick advanced forward until he was eighteen inches in front of Captain Posee's desk and came to attention. His eyes fixed firmly on the wall and twelve inches above the Captain's head, Kendrick barked, "Corporal Buck has reported as ordered, Sir."

"Instruct Corporal Buck to wait where he is. Call the MPs and have them escort Corporal Buck to the brig. Draft documents for Summary Court-martial. The charges to be Missing Movement."

Kendrick remained at rigid attention and said nothing until the Captain stared up at him and said, "Something on your mind, Corporal?"

"Request permission to speak freely."

"Speak."

"Sir, Buck's record is clean. He's a very short timer who is AWOL from liberty taken for the purpose of a job interview and who was not back on time because he was protecting his mother from a riot. Surely, Sir, Office Hours will do."

"Corporal Buck is not AWOL. When he accepted orders from the Recruiting Center in Memphis and missed the bus he missed a movement. For that offense Office Hours are not adequate."

"But, Captain...."

"That will be all, Kendrick. Call the MPs and fill out the Summary Court documents as instructed."

Kendrick rocked on his heels but didn't move.

"That will be all, Kendrick."

Kendrick executed an about-face and marched away from the Captain's desk. As he stepped through the door the Captain called after him.

"Kendrick. Tell Buck to step in."

"Aye, aye, Sir." He spoke without turning to face the Captain and continued walking.

When he reached his desk he looked down at Buck. "You heard him. Step in."

It was Buck's turn to stand in the middle of the opening and bang on the frame.

"Come."

Buck strode into the office and parked his frame eighteen inches from the Captain's desk; stood at attention with his eyes focused on the wall behind Captain Posee and twelve inches above the top of his head. "Corporal Buck reporting as ordered, Sir," he said in a slow, soft drawl.

"Corporal Buck you missed a movement when you chose not to get on that bus. Missing Movement is not Absent Without Leave and will not be treated like it. Do you understand?"

"Sir?"

"Buck, you were AWOL when you were late. But once you got those orders to get on the bus you ended your AWOL period. You knew that. That's why you did it."

"Yes, Sir."

"And then you violated those orders. Direct orders. You didn't get on the bus. That, Buck, is Missing Movement. Marines are not allowed to miss ships and they're not allowed to miss busses."

"Sir, I—"

"Stop. You'll get your say at your court-martial. That will be here. Tomorrow at eleven hundred hours. Do you want counsel? There is the potential of brig time so you may have it if you want it."

"Do I need it?"

"Buck, a Summary Court is you and me in this office. You may have counsel if you want it. If not it will be the two of us."

Corporal Buck continued at attention with his eyes above

the Captain's head as was required of him. "Like Office Hours, Sir."

"Yes, like Office Hours, except the penalties available to me are harsher than those in Office Hours."

"Like what, Sir?"

"As I said, the officer in charge of a Summary Court-martial may impose brig time. He may also impose lesser punishments including loss of rank, pay, and liberty."

Buck stood rigidly silent for moments. "Just you and me, Sir?"

"Just you and me, Buck."

"I'll do it that way, Sir."

"Buck, you will wait in the outer office until the MPs show up. They will escort you to the brig. When the charges are prepared, they will be read to you. You will be escorted from the brig back to this office in the morning, and we will proceed."

Silence ensued, broken by Rommel's yawn.

"Dismissed, Corporal Buck."

THERE was harmony to the footfalls in the corridor. With each stride two notes struck of an instant, the sound separate, not by time, but volume and pitch. One the sharp precise note of duty and the other a softer tone of resignation. Jack looked to see the open frame of the doorway filled with Buck's slim figure, hands cuffed together in front, followed immediately by a uniformed Marine wearing a white web belt and shoulder banner. The belt holstered both a side arm and a billy club. Large black block "MP" letters were stamped boldly across the face of the banner. The MP called Buck to such attention as his handcuffed arms would allow and looked at Lance Corporal Kendrick.

"Sergeant Oswald reporting as ordered with a detail of one. Sign here for receipt of the prisoner."

He handed a clipboard with the appropriate transmittal of Buck attached.

Kendrick stood, took the clipboard from the MP, and said, "Just a moment, Sergeant. I'll get the Captain's signature."

He stepped into the doorframe, requested and received permission to enter.

"Captain, the MP is here with Buck." He held forth the clipboard to the Captain, who scrawled his name across the signature block and handed it back.

"Send Corporal Buck in."

"Do you want the handcuffs removed, Sir?"

The Captain hesitated a moment as though he had not contemplated the thought and the responded softly, "Yes, have his handcuffs removed."

Jack stepped back into the outer office to see a glum Corporal Buck and his guard standing and filling the small space available between his desk and the file cabinets facing it. He handed the clipboard and signed receipt to the MP.

"Sergeant, the Captain requests Buck's handcuffs be removed."

The MP accepted the clipboard, put it under his left arm, opened the snap on a small leather pouch in front of the billy club ring on the left side of the web belt, and took out a key. Buck turned to face him, hands held forward. The MP fitted the key into the lock and released each cuff. He then removed the cuffs, put them into a leather pouch behind the pistol holster on the right rear of the web belt, put the key away, and left without a word.

Kendrick turned his eyes back toward Buck, who stood rubbing his wrists. They looked mutely at one another for a moment.

"Bud, I'm...."

"Don't say nuttin', College Boy. Nuttin' you can do."

With that he turned to the Captain's door, pulled himself to his full height, and knocked on the doorframe.

"Come."

Buck stepped in to meet his judgment.

"Scott, close the door behind Corporal Buck," came the disembodied command.

Sergeant Scott rose and did as instructed. Lance Corporal Kendrick sat down at his desk.

They waited.

NO more than twenty minutes passed from the time Scott closed the door until the Captain opened it. The shoulders of his stocky frame were pulled up and back into a forceful posture. With a rigid formality he extended Buck's record book to Sergeant Scott.

"Scott, prepare an order for my signature and as of this date showing William Buck's rank reduced to Lance Corporal."

As an expressionless Scott wordlessly accepted his order, Captain Posee looked at Kendrick and ordered, "Escort Lance Corporal Buck to the tailor and stay with him until appropriate insignia of rank is affixed to his uniform blouse."

Buck appeared behind the Captain. His shoulders pulled slightly forward and chin down. His face an obvious struggle to present a benign countenance.

— · —

THE two Lance Corporals sat on stools between the counter and the plate glass window at "Diamond Lou's," the tailor shop that took its name from the United States Marine Corps legendary Gunnery Sergeant Lou Diamond. Diamond was considered the perfect Marine in the era of the Banana Republic wars. Lance Corporal Buck was stripped to his T-shirt while the blouse of his uniform greens was having the two chevron insignia of his former rank replaced with the single chevron with the red rocker below, the insignia of his present rank, sewn on.

"Well, Buck, it isn't so bad. Nineteen days you're shit-out-of-here, back home, and promoted to civilian and working."

Buck sat quietly with his elbows on his knees and head hanging down. He raised his face without changing position and looked blankly at Kendrick. "Maybe, College Boy. Maybe."

He continued to hold Kendrick's eyes. "What you gonna do when you get out?"

"Drive that rusted out piece-of-shit Corvair van I bought from the Officers' Club back to L.A., if it makes it that far, grow some hair, and get a job."

"What sort of job?"

"Hadn't thought about it much. Whatever pays best I guess. After making eighty-four dollars a month, I'd like to drink call whiskey for a change."

"But you got choices."

Kendrick just looked at him, knowing he'd go on.

"See, Kendrick, I don't. When you're black with a high school education in Memphis, there ain't a lot."

"You got the G.I. Bill, Buck. You're smart. Go back to school, get a degree."

Buck let his head drop for a moment. When he looked back up there was a deep sadness in his black eyes. "I got Momma. That's good, but she takes care. I've been sending her fifty a month to live on. That barely gets her by. Now there's two of us." He paused. "Gotta work, Kendrick. Gotta work."

"Well you've got the job. Night shift super at three twenty-five an hour. It's a start."

"Do I? You think so? Make yourself the manager of that Hojos. You hired an NCO from the United States Marine Corps to ramrod that shift. Turns out the man got busted and is an enlisted man. Your offer still good?"

"Hey, Marine. Your blouse is ready." A potbellied tailor wearing a sweat-stained T-shirt stood at the counter, holding Buck's freshly pressed blouse with the Lance Corporal insignia newly attached.

Buck slowly rose and walked to the counter. He took the offered shirt, put it on, buttoned it up, and tucked it in with precise military pleats folded into the rear.

"Buck and a quarter, Marine."

Buck paid him and turned to face a now standing Kendrick.

"Now that you don't outrank me, okay if I call you William? Or is it Bill or Billy?"

"Why don't you call me Bud like always?"

Kendrick looked at his watch. "Okay, Bud, day's over. How about you join me at the 1–2–3 Club and let me buy you a beer?"

For the first time all afternoon Buck's resigned expression

gave way to a wan smile. "You're right, College Boy. No more NCO club for me. And that was my last folding money till payday. You buyin', I'm drinkin'."

IT was just before 1900 when the two Marines stepped out of the Quonset hut that was the 1–2–3 Club, the place set aside for Marines ranked E-1 through E-3, privates, PFCs, and lance corporals to drink cheap beers and eat stale pretzels at Maintenance Support Battalion. Neither was drunk but the two pitchers of beer had eased the wearing drama of the day. They stood in the gravel street at the base of the concrete steps in the gathering dark of the cold early spring evening. Quonset huts lined both sides of the street. Most had 100-watt incandescent light bulbs fitted into standard-issue hunter-green-metal shades. Each just beginning to cast a visible cone of light down onto the space below the doors. The light was strong enough to form shadows of the two Marines and a fifty-gallon galvanized-metal trash can just outside the door, the final receptacle of paper beer cups as Marines left the Club.

"Well if it isn't 'Lance Corporal' Buck!" a nasal voice snarled. Kendrick and Buck looked up to see Sergeant Townsend stride down the street toward them. "Single chevron looks right on you, Buck. You never were good enough for the second. I heard you lost it and couldn't wait to see for myself."

Neither Marine moved.

"Brace, asshole," Townsend demanded, looking directly at Buck.

"Lighten up, Townsend," Kendrick protested.

"You'll stay out of this, Kendrick, if you know what's good for you," Townsend growled, never taking his eyes off Buck. "Guess we won't be seeing you at the NCO Club for a final beer, will we?"

Buck stood loosely and said nothing. His dark countenance showed no expression at all.

"Seems to be true. Momma's boy just couldn't follow orders after all. That right, Lance Corporal?"

Townsend stopped less than a foot from Buck. Both men stared unblinking.

"Your dumb-ass nigger pals burn down their own neighborhood and Momma got scared? That it?"

Buck visibly stiffened, chin thrust forward, shoulders square, almost at attention.

Kendrick took one step toward them. "Sergeant, that's enough!"

Buck didn't move his eyes at all. "I got this, College Boy." It came out low and soft.

Townsend's face lifted into a grin. "You got nothin', Buck. You didn't help yourself, your momma, your 'home boys' or that rabble-rousing nigger, Dr. King."

Townsend never saw the punch that hit him in the belly. He doubled forward with a grunt. Buck grabbed both his ears and drove his head down as he lifted his knee to smash Townsend's nose and lips. Townsend was thrown back up with the force of the blow, staggered two steps, and crashed into the fifty-gallon trash can, spilling beer cups all over the street as it clattered and rolled over twice.

Townsend lay on his back, his cover gone and blood running down his face. Buck stood over him.

"Get up, Townsend. Get up and let's talk some more about niggers and Momma and Dr. King."

Townsend's boot caught Buck behind the knee and pulled him down. He rolled as he fell and landed on his hip and shoulder, bouncing back up as though he'd hit a trampoline instead of paper cups. He was on the balls of his feet, fists held low. Townsend staggered to rise, snarling through the blood coming out his nose.

Far away, Kendrick heard "Fight!" shouted through the still spring air. The door of the club opened and two Marines pushed to be the first out.

"Your rabble-rousing preacher got what he deserved, Buck, and so will you."

Townsend rushed like a bull pierced by the matador's blade but not yet down, head and shoulders low and blowing a froth of blood.

Buck veered left and drove a left fist into the side of Townsend's head as he went by. Townsend's momentum carried him forward two steps before he fell. He landed hard and rolled onto his back. Buck's scream was primal as he dove onto Townsend's chest and squatted with his knees on Townsend's shoulders. He swung with his right first. "For Momma!" Blood flew and Townsend's face snapped to the side with the force of the blow. "For the niggers!" Buck bellowed as his left fist snapped Townsend's face back. "And for Doctor," his right fist smashed, "Martin," the left, "Luther," the right, "King," the left, "Junior," the right.

Buck slowly rose and glared at the motionless and bloody figure spread-eagled on the ground before him.

THE BASIC SCHOOL
USMC BASE QUANTICO, VA
1630 15 APR 68

COMMANDING OFFICER
MAINTENANCE SUPPORT COMPANY
HEADQUARTERS AND SERVICE BATTALION

1) LANCE CORPORAL WILLIAM BUCK, HAVING BEEN
JUDGED THIS DATE BY A DULY AUTHORIZED
GENERAL COURTS MARTIAL FROM IN COMPLI-
ANCE WITH THE STANDARDS SPECIFIED IN THE
UNIFORM CODE OF MILITARY JUSTICE HAS BEEN
FOUND GUILTY OF THE OFFENSE OF STRIK-
ING A SUPERIOR, NAMELY SERGEANT SIMON
TOWNSEND AND SENTENCED AS FOLLOWS:

    A) SHALL BE REDUCED IN RANK TO PRIVATE

    B) SHALL SERVE TWO YEARS HARD LABOR AND
       CONFINEMENT

    C) SHALL BE DISHONORABLY DISCHARGED
       FROM THE UNITED STATES MARINE CORPS.

2) YOU ARE HEREBY ORDERED TO MAKE APPRO-
PRIATE NOTIFICATION TO PVT. BUCK'S SERVICE
RECORD.

3) YOU ARE HEREBY ORDERED TO TURN PVT
BUCK OVER TO THE BASE PROVOST FOR TRANS-
PORT TO US NAVAL PRISON, PORTSMOUTH, NEW
HAMPSHIRE.

BY DIRECTION OF BASE COMMANDER
LTGEN H. MELVILL

Roundtree's Coming

Tuesday April 16, 1968

JACK LOOKED AT his watch—0755. He knew just where to go. If he got to the middle of the grinder between the two classroom buildings, he might catch one late and running for class. Bastards might be officers but they were still students with students' motivations and concerns. Sometimes they got late and running, fearful of not being on time. And sometimes they forgot. You never could tell. He might just get lucky and catch one.

He positioned himself in the middle of the asphalt grinder. Some hundred yards in front of him a long, two-story, red-brick building lined one end of the parade ground. Its mate, another hundred yards behind him, lined the other end. One minute to eight and the four acres were vacant, except for him—him and the Lieutenant in green fatigues who came running out the door, head down, and pumping for the classroom on the other side.

It took just a few steps to get directly into his path and wait. Four, three, two.… He braced rigidly at attention and raised the index finger of his stiffened right hand to the bill of his cover.

Head down, the Lieutenant stormed past.

He held the salute and pivoted toe and heel to face the racing officer's back and bellowed, "LIEUTENANT!"

It was a perfect copy of the tone used by drill instructors to shout, "PRIVATE" at any recruit they wished to intimidate.

He swore he could see the rubber burn off the heels of the young Marine officer's boots as he went from full run to full stop and then braced to attention and pivoted to face the voice.

He enjoyed the complexity of the officer's expression as he realized he faced only a Lance Corporal. He milked the moment as long as he could, knowing that if he played it out too long the officer would take the offensive.

"Sir," he barked. "This Marine has saluted a Marine officer and that salute rates a return." And then added the final, *de rigueur* "Sir."

In the end, he knew the Lieutenant's fear would win out over his anger.

The Lieutenant returned his salute, dropped it, and then with as much dignity as he could muster turned and walked toward his classroom.

Jack allowed the full expression of his joy to glow on the retreating officer. And if he were reprimanded for his tardiness, well, maybe the officer should have thought of that before he'd used up all his time.

— · —

"YOU look like the cat who just ate the canary, Kendrick."

Jack Kendrick hung his starched and pressed utility cover over the peg on the wall, slid into the chair behind his desk, and removed the dust cover from his typewriter.

"Captain Posee in yet?" He nodded to the open door between the office he and Sergeant Scott shared and the company commander's office.

"Not yet. We can talk."

"You're right about the look. Just caught a young lieutenant, rushing head down across the grinder, who was in too big a hurry to return my salute."

"And?"

"It was my pleasure to instruct him in proper Marine Corps protocol."

"And thereby make him late for class, knowing that the result of his transgression would be a severe ass-chewing by some captain instructor?"

"Serving in a battalion with 1,500 student lieutenants is a pain in the ass, Scotty. I get tired of walking down the road saluting a parade of passing trainees. Besides,..." Kendrick looked toward the open door. "...today I think all officers are pricks."

Scott's look was solemn. "You're not the only one pissed about Buck, you know."

"I'm sure that's true, but damn, I feel helpless. He was a good Marine who didn't ask for much and got fucked by The Corps."

"You heard what happened last night?"

Kendrick sat up from his typewriter and turned his chair to face Scott. "No. What?"

"They shut down the 1–2–3 Club and the NCO Club last night."

"Why?"

"Fights."

"Drunk Marines fighting. There's news."

"It is if it takes up half the club and all the guys on one side are black and all the guys on the other side white."

"No shit!" Kendrick's eyes widened. "Why? Buck?"

"Who knows? Buck? Martin Luther King? Black Panthers?" Scott paused. "Who knows, Kendrick? It's all over America, and it appears the United States Marine Corps is not immune."

"What's he going to do?" Kendrick nodded his head toward the open door.

"It's way above the company level. It will be battalion level at least. Maybe the whole base. That's where he is now. Colonel called an 0700 meeting of all company commanders. We'll know soon enough."

"Any guesses?"

"Yeah," Scott said. "I hear Roundtree's coming."

"Who?"

"The legendary Master Gunnery Sergeant Louis Roundtree. I think the battalion is getting a new top sergeant."

"Scotty, he may be legendary, but I have no idea who you're talking about."

"Top Roundtree was the first black man in the United States Marine Corps to win a Navy Cross. He was a cook, just like our guys, in Korea. And just like you, he was a young corporal, running a field mess at Pork Chop Hill. Story is he was in the kitchen when the Chi-Coms started blowing their bugles.

By the time he got outside, the bad guys had penetrated the perimeter and were rushing in. He swapped his skillet for a BAR he picked up from some dead Marine and started killing gooks. And he held up. Some other guys formed around him, and next thing you know a rout became an orderly retreat. He gave ground very slowly and was about the last guy off the Hill."

"Some Marine."

"Yeah, Kendrick, some Marine. Still is. I've seen him. All spit and polish and, from what I hear, hard as nails. And he's black and he started in a Marine Corps kitchen. If anybody can put a lid on this thing it's Roundtree."

THE entire battalion stood in formation, in dress greens and at attention on the grinder. From his position in the front row of Maintenance Support Company, Corporal Kendrick could see the Colonel walking slowly across the front of the battalion formation. He was followed by his adjutant and one other Marine—not an officer but a Master Gunnery Sergeant. Kendrick and every other Marine in the battalion knew this wasn't the Colonel's inspection. It was for "Top" Roundtree to review his new charges.

As they drew closer Kendrick took his eyes off the reviewing party and brought them full front. He, like every other Marine here, had pressed his greens, cleaned his rifle until not one spec of lint showed down the bore, and polished everything that would shine—shoes, brass buttons, belt buckle, even the bill of his barracks cover—until he could see his blue eyes reflecting back at him. He knew better than to call attention to himself by being at other than perfect attention with eyes front. The Colonel and his adjutant strode by without pause. Master Gunnery Sergeant Roundtree did not.

Roundtree stopped and inspected him from shoe tips up. He stopped and gazed into Kendrick's face. There was no eye contact, because Kendrick's eyes were focused rigidly at the colors across the grinder. But Jack saw him. He was a poster model of a squared-away Marine. Roundtree's uniform was perfect in every detail, no seam or button out of place; and his posture suggested his spine was not only perfectly erect but had never touched the back of a chair. The ribbons on his left lapel covered every campaign since World War II and extended up his lapel almost to his collarbone. The top row was a single ribbon, which Jack recognized as the navy blue with a white vertical stripe of a Navy Cross. The black face showed no expression. This was not a man trying to be hard. It was the face of competence, of a man who had all the tools of command and knew just how and when to use each. It was a face that immediately reminded Jack of Hemingway's simple and profound description of courage. It was "grace under pressure."

Jack Kendrick found himself seeing five feet, seven inches and one hundred forty pounds of perfect Marine.

"MAINTENANCE Support Company, Sergeant Scott speaking, Sir."

There was a long pause.

"Yes, Sergeant Roundtree. Immediately." Scott hung up the phone. "Top Roundtree wants you in his office."

"What for, Scotty?"

"He didn't say. Something administrative I suppose."

— · —

THE nameplate on the closed door read, "Master Gunnery Sergeant Louis Roundtree." Kendrick pounded sharply on the doorframe, twice.

After several seconds of silence his knock was answered with a soft but direct, "Come."

Kendrick opened the door and faced into a utilitarian ten by twelve–foot space. Roundtree sat behind a small wooden desk directly in front of him. His benign expression gave away nothing as he looked directly at Jack.

"Step in and close the door, Corporal."

Kendrick did as instructed.

"Scott said you wanted to see me, Master Gunnery Sergeant."

"I need you to prepare an order for Captain Posee's signature."

Jack waited.

"Sergeant Townsend will be back on full duty today."

It was a statement, not a question.

"He will be reassigned to WestPac immediately. Prepare the usual order. He will have five days' transit time to San Diego and he may take up to thirty days' leave, if he has it coming, on his way."

Jack's face lit with a small grin.

"Something bothering you, Kendrick?"

"No, Master Gunnery Sergeant, it is not."

"See that it's on the Captain's desk within the hour."

JACK'S step was light as he walked into his office. He opened a file cabinet, pulled the appropriate form, sat down, and spun it into his typewriter.

"What'd Top want?" Scott asked.

"It seems that Sergeant Townsend is going to Viet Nam."

"JESUS, Kendrick, look at that squall line roll up the hill," Scott said, pointing.

Kendrick walked across the office to peer out the window next to Sergeant Scott's desk. The sky to the east was almost black where there should have been late-April sunshine. Exactly as Scott had said, the squall was rolling up the hill, coming fast, dumping torrents of rain on everything below it.

"God damn, I'm tired of this cold, miserable spring. Northern Virginia should be basking in warmth by now. Hell, I should be basking in warmth by now," Scott muttered.

Kendrick involuntarily shivered. "I am so tired of freezing in that damn Greenbrier. Floorboard below the driver's seat is so rusted out you can see pavement while you drive."

"Well, tonight you'll be able to see the water that's rushing up from the highway before it soaks your utilities. Won't that be nice?" Scotty asked.

"Scotty, I'm so far behind it's going to be another four or five hours before I have to dodge raindrops. Storm might have passed by then."

"If you're lucky, Kendrick. If you're lucky."

HE wasn't.

It was a little after 2000 hours when Kendrick snapped off the light and closed the office door. He said goodnight to the duty sergeant before he left company HQ and stood at the door watching water pour out of the sky. The twenty-knot wind behind it blew the raindrops in at a forty-five-degree angle. He'd made a mistake that morning and left the apartment without a field jacket. He pulled his starched utility cover down tight, slammed the door behind him, and took off at a run for the parking lot on the other side of the battalion area. It would be more than a mile.

It took Kendrick ten minutes to get there. He was drenched to the skin when he did, and his cover was a limp, unstarched mess. He pulled the key out of his pocket as he tried to sprint the last fifty yards across the unpaved mud puddle that was the NCO lot. He fumbled the key toward the door lock. It slipped out of his fingers and fell soundlessly into the mud somewhere at his feet. He bent over in the dark and felt around in the slop for it. The key wasn't where he thought it should be, so he got on his knees. His two minutes on his hands and knees digging through three inches of mud were finally rewarded.

By the time he opened the door and seated himself behind the wheel he was shivering. The engine turned over on the second try. A very cold wind blew up through the holes where there should have been floorboard. Much as he wanted heat, there was no point in even turning it on until the engine had warmed. By the time he merged onto I-95 northbound to D.C. he was shivering, but the engine heat display was up, so he turned it on. Now he had heat rushing up from the ventilator to go with the cold air rushing up through the holes below him.

He also turned on the radio. His soaked cotton utilities clung to him and seemed to transmit more cold than heat to his entire body. His boots were soaked and his toes felt frozen.

What was Chesty Puller's famous line from Korea? "*Cold makes cowards of us all.*" *Well, God damn it, I'm a coward right now.*

But the headlights and the wipers worked, and it seemed almost no other fools were heading into D.C. in the storm. If he could find a place on the street to park this piece of shit of a Corvair he'd be home in a hot shower within forty-five minutes. He settled into a managed state of misery and stared at what little he could see of the highway.

"And for those of you who are tired of miserable weather, we've got Mama Cass Elliott and the Mamas and the Papas agreeing with you. Here's their hit 'California Dreamin',"" the rock-jock announced. "This will be just right for a cold night in the District."

All the leaves are brown and the sky is gray.

They had Jack's attention on the first line.

I've been for a walk on a winter's day.
I'd be safe and warm if I was in L.A.
California Dreamin' on such a winter's day.

Jack's mind was as numb as his body. He just drove.

THE alarm went off at 0500. It was pitch black in the basement. He was warm, here under the blanket, curved into the small of her back. He extended an arm from under the cover into the cold and shut off the alarm, but he didn't get up. He just lay there listening to the rain pounding on the street and to the tree limbs banging into one another.

Going to be complete fucking misery out there. Tree limbs everywhere and every low intersection between here and the

Potomac flooded. How the hell am I going to get to work? Fuck work! Fuck the United States Marine Corps. I'm warm here and I'm safe here. I'm not going to work.

He pulled his arm back under the cover, rolled toward Jasmine's back, reached over her body and slowly stroked her belly.

"Ummm," she purred.

He took it as an invitation but didn't accept. He just lay there in the dark—warm and safe.

LIGHT crept in through the slats in the half-basement blinds. It was soft and shadowless. Jasmine stood over him, a steaming mug in her hand. Her other stroked his crew cut. The folds of her unsashed robe hung open, but the light was behind her and all he could see inside the robe was mysterious welcoming shadow.

"Your duty calls, Warrior Prince." She sat on the edge of the bed and extended the mug toward him.

"Your warrior prince is tired of duty."

"Now that's the most sensible thing you've said since we met."

Jack smiled.

"My hippie lifestyle starting to win you over, is it?" She dropped her hand from his head down under the cover and ran her nails through the hair on his chest. "If it feels good, do it."

"That an offer or a statement of the philosophy which you think is winning me over, Jas?"

"Both," she said as she set the mug of tea on the packing crate they used for a bedside table. She leaned closer, her head still above his, until a smoothly rounded breast took form in the shadow of her robe. She lowered it toward his mouth and he kissed it, more dutifully than passionately.

"My warrior really is down this morning, isn't he?" She sat back up and reached behind herself for the mug, but didn't close the robe.

Her outline was no longer solid black. He could now see her eyes and lips partially formed in the burgeoning light. He could also see wisps of hair forming a halo around her head and mist rising above the mug as she lifted it to her lips.

She patted his shoulder and stood up. "All right, if you're not going to accept the best offer you'll get all day, time to get up, get out there in the storm, and go defend me from the Communist menace."

"No. I'm going to sleep in today." He rolled over on his side his back to the window.

"You mean it." She was surprised.

JACK drifted back off and was awakened from dreams of volleyball on the beach by a gentle kiss on the forehead. There was now enough light leaking in between the slats in the blind for him to see a very pretty young woman, no make-up on. Her hair, combed down long, spread around the shoulders of a navy-blue crew-necked sweater.

"That mine?"

"Army gear is in style in my set, WP."

"Marine Corps, Jas. Marine Corps. But I gotta admit I never saw a Marine look that good in a sweater."

She smiled. "I've got early shift at the co-op. Since I can't live on the eighty-four bucks a month you bring in, I gotta go. And you, Warrior, should probably get your ass outta bed and get to work before the USMC has very harsh things to say about your tardiness."

Jack reached out a hand and stuck his finger though the belt loop of her jeans. "Too late to accept that offer?"

"Way late!" She spun away, grabbed a hooded jacket and an umbrella off the rack, and opened the door. Wind and rain blew in. She stepped out, but before closing the door her head reappeared. "See you this evening or when they let you out of jail, whichever comes first," she said, and then disappeared.

Jack shouted at the closed door. "The brig, Jas. It's called a brig."

HE was awakened by the silence. No rain, no wind, just stillness and warm spring light trying to batter down the shutters. Naked, he rose from bed, took two steps to the door, and opened it, making certain only his head showed to passersby on 21st Street who might be looking down the half-flight of stairs from the street to his door.

The day was magnificent—sunny and already sixty-five degrees, with only enough wind to stir the air and give him his second good-morning kiss. He resisted the temptation to step onto the street stark naked, stretch, yawn, and scream, "Good morning!" to the world. But he closed the door and did the rest standing in his room.

Naked, Jack walked around the bed and picked his still wet utilities up from the vinyl and chrome kitchen chair that served for both table and guest seating. The room came with a credenza so big that he'd never been able to figure how they got it down there. It was carved linden wood with spiraled legs four inches thick spinning up from the layer of drawers along the floor and supporting a magnificent polished top, with more drawers and a mirrored centerpiece.

His Salvation Army fold-out couch, round Formica and chrome kitchen table, and two chairs didn't seem out of place with the credenza. In its presence you just didn't notice the rest.

Jack stuffed his hand into the left front pocket of the utilities and pulled out four soggy bills—a five and three ones. The right front pocket produced a quarter and two dimes—eight dollars and forty-five cents. He had gas and tomorrow was payday.

Well, payday or the brig. If the former I'll have eighty-four bucks and if the latter I won't need any. The United States Marine Corps will be caring for all my creature needs. So I've got $8.45 to blow and a magnificent day to do it.

It took Jack forty-five minutes to shower, shave, put on jeans and a work shirt, stuff the covers on top of the bed and fold the thing into a sofa, and then hang his soggy utility uniform on the line over the trash cans in the area outside the back door.

Okay, Jack, let's go enjoy our nation's capital.

THE coffee, toasted bagel, and cream cheese cost sixty-two cents, and both filled and warmed him. The walk to the tidal basin took twenty-five minutes. Jefferson was always a bit too eloquent for Jack but always made him smile.

Tommy sure had a beautiful way with words, but never seemed quite real. Too academic and philosophical. Lincoln's more my style. Pithy. But Jefferson will be a good place to start.

It was the outside of the monument that impressed him

the most. The Potomac this morning was dark brown, almost black with eroded soil, and it swirled in an angry, defiant way, making the point that the sea wall behind the monument wouldn't hold it back forever.

Someday, Jack thought, *it will pull down the pilings and the wall and eat away the raised soil packed in behind them, eventually washing under the foundations and pulling down the beautiful and tranquil domed monument that is our reverent tribute to our native son who outshone all the European Enlightenment intellectuals. When will that be? Four hundred years from now? A thousand years? Fifty years?*

Who can know? Someday, but not today. Today humanity reigns over this spot and offers it in tribute to one of our best.

Had the storm come three weeks later, the white blossoms of the cherry trees around the monument would have littered the ground in the sad confetti of failed promise. Now just a few limbs had been broken and the nascent buds were still in place, and the Potomac's anger aside, the monument and grounds were washed clean. And the tidal basin, which swept from the Potomac around two sides of the monument, was still. Here the darkness of the water didn't look angry. It was shimmerless and shiny, the water holding the mysterious promise of black glass. It hid what could not yet be seen with inviting luster, not of opacity, but a translucence which could not quite be penetrated.

Yes, Jefferson was a very good place to start.

I wonder what Tommy would have done about Buck?

And as soon as he asked himself the answer came.

Mr. "All men are created equal" would have done nothing, because he was also so frightened of the prospect of millions of freed but unassimilated, uneducated, or unacculturated Negroes being unleashed on America that he never even freed those he could have, his own, including some of his own sons. No help for Buck here.

Lincoln was always Jack's favorite, *'cause he's like me. Grew up without money, status, connections, or any power but his own. But he was free and made something of himself. And one of the things he made of himself was wise. I wonder if I'll ever get there. And he had great strength, enough to carry the whole Union when it could not carry itself. And despite that he never lost his humility or faith in Americans.*

A brisk ten-minute walk and Jack stood staring up at the gaunt, haunted, and haunting face of the greatest American. After a quick nod "Hello," he raced up the stairs so he could stand behind Abe's statue and read the two greatest short speeches he'd ever heard or read. And he reread them. On the left wall Lincoln's great paean to both the Gettysburg Union dead and the idea for which they gave "their last full measure," and on the right his humble plea for forgiveness for their killers—his Second Inaugural address, "…with malice toward none and charity for all…."

Here is a man, a leader, worth dying for.
I wonder if Buck would agree?

And again the answer came instantly.

Buck die for the man who said, "I would free some of the slaves, all of the slaves, none of the slaves, if it would save the Union"? Probably not.

That realization brought a slow and chastened cadence to the footfalls that only moments before had raced up the steps to the Lincoln Memorial as they started back down. Halfway down the steps Jack stopped and lifted his eyes. The white obelisk of the Washington Monument standing erect and phallic above the skyline at the other end of the Mall, commanding all in its splendid isolation, could not be ignored. Jack grinned at a thought he was certain had been shared by thousands of others.

He's the father of a whole nation. What else should his monument be if not a giant phallus?

Jack walked slowly across the street, entered the Mall, and strolled along the edge of the reflecting pool toward Washington's monument.

Of the three he was the warrior, and in his case Jasmine's "Warrior Prince" fits. If not the richest man in America, he was one of them. Patrician, married money, speculated on land well and wisely, and became the largest landowner and distiller in America.

And fearless. Soldier from his youth in the French and Indian War. Alleged to be psychotically indifferent to his personal safety and gunfire as a field commander, and, as a general who'd suffered nothing but losses from Boston to New York and south though New Jersey, was unafraid to take an ill-nourished and ill-equipped band of survivors across a stormy Delaware River and march all night in freezing rain to take on the terror of European mercenaries, the Hessians, and kick their ass.

The only thing I've ever heard he was afraid of was being buried alive. Insisted, several times, on allowing "a decent interval" to pass between his death and his burial.

He walked all the way to the monument and looked up from its base. In that attitude Washington commanded not only the earth but the heavens as well. Jack looked upward reverently for a long time.

And this one freed his slaves. Buck woulda had a chance with him. A warrior who wasn't afraid.

THE gallon jug of Red Mountain wine cost $4.32 tax included. That left Jack eighty-four cents until payday or the brig. Hopefully, Jasmine had brought dinner makings home from the co-op. And if not, "Man cannot live by bread alone."

She had, and when Jack walked in the door he was met by the smells of frying sausage and onions with a hint of warming marinara sauce wafting at the edges of olfactory sensitivity. Spaghetti with sausages and enough wine to close off awareness. Perfect.

IT was dark or almost so. They'd never turned the lights on. He could not only see the silhouette of the gallon jug but also make out that nearly half of the wine was gone. He sat at one end of the couch, his hip pushed against the arm. She had her head in his lap and her legs stretched along the length of the couch. It was silent in their basement and had been for several minutes.

"Jack.... Honey, are you going back?"

"I don't know."

His right hand lazily stroked her ear and the edge of her face. She kissed his thumb.

"I don't know, Jas. I know I don't want to."

"What then? Come to work at the co-op?"

"Maybe back home. L.A. Just disappear."

"Disappear? Won't they look for you?"

He took a long drink from the glass he held in his left hand. "If I can find work, I'm not sure they'll know."

"How do you find work without a Social Security number?"

"Raise your head a minute, Jas. Let me get the jug."

She sat half up and he slid out from under her head. With his butt propped on the edge of the couch he reached for the jug and poured his glass full again.

"Want another?"

"I've still got plenty. Just scoot back so I can drop my head."

He did and she did. He was silent for a long time in the dark.

"There's always Canada," he finally said.

"Remember the day we met, Jack?"

He ran his hand across her sweater and stroked her breast. "Of course I remember."

Jasmine giggled. "Not that, silly. Before that. By the reflecting pool in front of Lincoln."

"Yeah, Honey, I remember that too."

"Do you remember what you asked Shaggy?"

"Shaggy?"

"About Socrates, Jack. You asked him if he knew what Socrates said about duty. And then you gave him part of the answer. That when the polis called, a man had only two choices."

She dropped her hand to the edge of the couch, picked up her glass, sat up part-way, took a drink, and set it back down. When she had her head nestled back in Jack's lap she continued.

"When I came back to you I asked what the two choices were. You never answered. I want to know."

It was pitch black in the apartment now. He sat quietly enveloped in it for a long time.

"Socrates said when the polis called a man had to answer

or stand in the town square and say, 'I won't' and take whatever punishment was meted out. That's why he drank the hemlock. Everyone thought he'd bribe his way out of jail and run to Thebes. That's what they expected. But he wouldn't run."

THE alarm went off at 0500. It took thirty minutes for him to shower, shave, and dress in what would be the uniform of the day, utilities. Before going to bed he had pressed his utilities, shined his boots, polished all his brass, and starched and pressed his utility cover. He'd have to face the music today. It was the only way he knew to prepare.

Jack shut off the light before stepping out of the bathroom, then walked soundlessly across the room, past the bed, and to the door.

No reason to wake her.

As he opened the door she spoke to him in a sleepy voice. "Call me when you can, W.P."

He smiled and nodded, not knowing if she could see, closed the door and walked up the half-flight of stairs to the darkened street.

He drove with the radio off, alone with nothing but the highway noise to comfort his fears. He had to face them; the distraction of music wouldn't help.

It started like this with Buck. Just AWOL. That's all. A simple AWOL, and the Marine Corps ground him to dust. What happens to me?

Jack stared straight ahead. Stars still shone in front of him. To the east the black of night was giving way to a flat gray of pre-dawn. No warmth in it, but the stars were going out and now warning clouds could be seen. Just gray.

Jasmine was right, of course. Where she led me. I really don't have any choices now. I've already made my choice—a piss-poor one. But it's done. Now they get to choose.

THE NCO lot had dried out. It was still muddy, but firm mud, not slop. He parked and started the mile walk up the hill. The sun was visible now; no real warmth from it, but light. He shivered, not knowing if it was cold or dread. A company of lieutenants marched down the street toward him on their way to chow. He saluted and kept walking, his right arm raised with stiff fingers touching the brim of his cover, and held it as he walked up the hill and they marched down.

As he stepped into his office, the light was on and Sergeant Scott was sitting behind his desk. Scott looked at him, a bland expression on his face, as Jack hung his cover on the peg, sat down at his desk, and removed the dust cover from his typewriter. The clock showed exactly 0700.

"Enjoy your holiday, Corporal Kendrick?" he finally asked.

"Not really," Kendrick responded.

"I suspect you'll enjoy today even less."

Jack turned and looked steadily into Scott's face. "I'm pretty sure you're right, Scotty. But nothing to be done about it now, is there?"

Scott returned the steady look but said nothing.

Jack turned back to his desk, picked up the first item in his in-box, spun it into the typewriter carriage, and started to work. There was nothing to do but work and wait.

And wait he did. The sun moved up above the window until it no longer cast harsh shadows across the office. Jack worked steadily, methodically on yesterday's business stacked up and waiting. He didn't leave for coffee. He just waited, and worked. He and Sergeant Scott didn't speak.

He hoped working would relieve his worry. But it wasn't sweat-inducing hard labor, the kind that would clear a man's mind and, at least for the moment, his soul; so it didn't. He found this work and worry were not mutually exclusive. The silence, broken by nothing but the clatter of keys and the periodic ding of an extended carriage, actually fed his self-absorption and the fear it carried with it.

It was exactly 1000 when Scott's phone rang. His response, "Yes, Top," told Jack it was Roundtree's line he'd answered. Scott said it again, "Yes, Top," and hung up.

"Roundtree wants to see you, Jack." His voice was soft but it carried no warmth.

Jack stopped typing, left the document on the carriage, and rose. He pulled himself to his full height and slowly placed his chair squarely in front of his desk. He stepped out the door, turned left into the hallway, took four paces to the first door on his right, squared his shoulders to it, came to the position of attention, and rapped twice on the frame.

"Come!"

He opened the door to see the figure of Master Gunnery Sergeant Roundtree sitting behind the desk directly in front of him. Roundtree was studying a folio on the desktop before him, but even doing that he was not bent. The Top sat erect, his spine not touching the back of his chair, his head erect, and only his eyes looking down his nose to the document. Jack strode as crisply as he could to a position eighteen inches in front of the desk, fixed his eyes on a spot on the wall twelve inches above Roundtree's head, and tried to bark rather than croak, "Master Gunnery Sergeant Roundtree, Corporal Kendrick reporting as ordered!"

There was no response. With his eyes fixed on the wall he couldn't be certain, but he had no indication Roundtree had picked his eyes up from the document he was studying. Kendrick remained frozen. And then he realized he had to breathe, and tried to do so without an exhale that would show his fear. He stood braced at attention without response, focusing all his energy on not moving his feet or the fingers pressed against the seams of his utility trousers. It was a long time.

The words came evenly, precisely, and at an unexpectedly conversational volume.

"Kendrick, if you ever have to do that again, you call me."

Jack didn't respond. He didn't know how to respond. His understanding came too slowly.

"Kendrick, that was an order. You do know the proper response from a Marine to a superior's order, do you not? It's 'Aye, aye,' meaning, 'I have heard and I will comply.'"

Jack found suddenly that he had saliva enough to lubricate his tongue. "Aye, aye, Master Gunnery Sergeant."

He knew far better than to allow even a hint of a smile to cross his face.

"And, Corporal Kendrick, take this to Sergeant Scott for Captain Posee's signature."

Kendrick looked down to see the brilliant, black expressionless face of Master Gunnery Sergeant Roundtree, his arm extended toward him with a folio in his hand.

Jack reached forward and grasped it.

"Dismissed, Kendrick."

"Aye, aye, Master Gunnery Sergeant."

Jack pointed the toe of his shoe onto the deck behind him, executed an about-face, and walked out.

Standing in the hallway, Jack looked at the folio. The third cut tab was neatly labeled "Kendrick, John C., Corporal." It was his folio and he opened it. The document lying in the middle was an authorization for leave. It was filled out authorizing Corporal John C. Kendrick one day's leave—yesterday.

California Dreamin'

"KENDRICK, I'M TYPING your promotion order," Scott said.

"Promotion!" Jack responded. "What promotion?"

"To civilian, Corporal Kendrick. To civilian."

Jack just grinned. It was a large, self-satisfied grin that said, *I've made it. My part's done. I'm out of here with both honor and sanity.*

"It is your order to Inactive Reserve. Absent we go to war someplace else with the Communist menace, you'll never hear from the Marine Corps until…" Sergeant Scott paused to look back into Kendrick's folio lying open on his desk. "…about April of 1972, at which point you will receive, quietly and without ceremony, and in the U.S. mail, an Honorable Discharge."

"After which point I will not care whether the Marine

Corps is ordered into defense against any menace—Communist or otherwise."

"Bingo!" Scott responded. "Last chance to change your Home of Record," he added. "Six cents a mile, paid in advance to get you home."

"I'll stick with L.A. The 150 bucks will buy gas if that piece-of-shit Greenbrier holds together. But I'm not sure it's enough for oil. Uses almost as much oil as gas."

Scott chuckled. "Princess Moonbeam going home with you?"

Kendrick swiveled his chair to face his office mate during these last fourteen months. "Jas and I have talked about this. A lot. We've been good for each other, but we were way stations for each other and we both know it."

"What the hell does that mean?"

Jack smiled. "I, Mr. Scott, before I was waylaid by a sense of honor—or was it adventure—and joined the Marine Corps, was a college grad with a yen to buy a house in the suburbs, get married, have two point four children, join the great American middle class, and perhaps, just perhaps, get sloppy rich."

"Noble aspirations all."

"Well, Jasmine, or Princess Moonbeam as you insist on calling her, shares none of them. She is a free spirit with no desire to be constrained by objectives and no fear of the future."

"So you're just going to leave her?"

"Not like you do it in North Dakota, is it, Scotty?"

The sergeant nodded.

"Jas and I have been good companions this last year. I'm her Warrior Prince phase."

"And what is she to you?"

"A sweet girl with beautiful tits who warms my bed but is not the companion of my life's work."

"I'll ask it again," Scott said. "You're just going to leave her?"

"Tonight I suspect she'll cook dinner. We'll share a little cheap wine, a joint or two, and great, goodbye sex. I've paid the rent through the end of next month for her. We'll both promise to write soon as we settle into new addresses, and it will never happen. Anything else, Scotty?"

Scott's face was rigid in a judgmental stare and then it broke and he laughed. "You're right, Jack. Not like we do it in North Dakota."

Jack shared the laugh.

"And, yes, there are a couple of other things." Scott picked up an eight-and-a-half by eleven–inch sheet of paper from his desk and handed it to Jack. "Your Exit Interview List. Spend the rest of the day getting each one of these to sign you out and be back here at 0800 tomorrow. I'll have your DD214 authorized by the Skipper along with a final pay voucher. You can take the voucher to the bank on base for cash, and you'll be outta here—free as a bird."

Jack looked at the Exit Interview List—Rifle Range (all weapons returned), Career Counseling (want to re-up?), and about two dozen other offices on base whose release he'd require.

"Scotty, I'll bet I've given this form to at least a hundred guys. Never contemplated what a real pain in the ass this would be. Very much like ensuring I didn't have any books checked out of the high school library before they gave me my diploma."

"Same thing exactly. Have fun."

Kendrick pulled his cover off the peg and stepped out of the office.

"See you in the morning, short-timer," Scott called after him.

"OKAY, Marine, what do you want to do with your uniforms?" the supply sergeant asked.

"That, Sergeant, is a question I've been waiting to answer for a long time," Kendrick responded as he hoisted his sea bag up onto the counter separating them. "I'll keep the utilities I've got on so as not to get busted for being out of uniform in the next..." He paused to look at his watch. "...twenty hours and fourteen minutes. You can have the rest."

Jack released the draw string on the top of the sea bag, turned it upside-down, and dumped the contents. "It's all there. Every uniform the United States Marine Corps has ever issued me."

"That attached to The Corps are you?" the supply sergeant asked with a grin, as he looked at the precisely folded uniforms now fallen into a loose heap on his counter.

"I'll keep the sea bag. I'll need something to carry all those worldly goods I've collected on the eighty-four dollars per month The Corps generously supplied me with since I made corporal."

Jack waited as the sergeant counted and enumerated each item of uniform clothing and dutifully noted each on form NAVMC 604-SD, Combined Individual Clothing Requisition, and Issue Slip (Men's), which he then signed and handed to him.

"Corporal, you ever get called up from Inactive this will get you new uniforms, so hang onto it."

Jack face flooded with an expression of mock sincerity. "Sergeant, during my two years, no Chinese Communists invaded Long Beach. If needed again the Marine Corps can count on me. Now do me the favor of signing the one I really need." Jack reached into his shirt pocket and pulled out the neatly folded Exit Interview List. He unfolded it and, with great ceremony, extended it to the NCO across the counter. "Yours is the last signature required to get me out of here."

The supply sergeant scrawled his signature and returned the form. Jack refolded it and restored it to the safety of his shirt pocket, picked up his now empty sea bag, and departed.

June 28, 1969

JACK arrived at the NCO lot at the bottom of the hill thirty minutes early. He'd filled the tank on the way out from the District. He had six quarts of oil and a spout in a cardboard box in the back of the van. His sea bag, the only other item in the back, lay only half full beside it.

After he'd parked and shut off the engine, Jack pulled a pack of Camels from his shirt pocket and shook one out. Once he'd put the cigarette between his lips and the pack back in his pocket, he arched up in the seat and pulled the Zippo from the pocket of his utility trousers. He lit the cigarette, inhaled deeply, then pushed out a long stream of smoke and put the lighter away.

Last time I'll make this walk up the hill and I won't miss it at all, he thought without a trace of nostalgia or sentiment. He sat quietly enjoying his smoke. On his last drag he exhaled a perfectly round smoke ring, flipped the butt out the window, rolled the window up, and got out.

His leisurely stroll up the hill was interrupted by a company of lieutenants being marched to chow hall coming toward him. He raised himself more erect, stiffened his stride and brought the fingers of his right hand to the brim of his utility cover. When the lieutenants passed he dropped his hand and loosened his posture.

It's Pavlovian. Soon enough I can start to unlearn.

"IT'S zero 800, Scotty. Got my DD214 and pay voucher, like you promised?"

"You've got one last task, Kendrick. Captain Posee is in." Scott nodded toward the open interoffice door. "He wants to see you."

Jack laid his utility cover on top of his desk—*Well, it used to be my desk*—shrugged, walked to the open door, squared his shoulders into the frame, and knocked twice on the jamb.

"Come."

Jack strode to the spot eighteen inches in front of the desk, noticing the white German Shepherd asleep on the mat in the corner. He came to attention, eyes rigidly fixed on the wall twelve inches above the Captain's head.

"Corporal Kendrick reporting as ordered, Sir!"

The Captain looked up a smile on his face. "At ease, Corporal."

Jack spread his feet to shoulder width and eased his posture.

"Kendrick, you have served me and this company for over

a year and your nation for almost two. I just wanted to offer you my thanks for that service."

"Thank you, Sir."

Captain Posee rose, leaned forward and extended his hand across the desk and added, "And wish you well in your future endeavors."

Jack looked at the extended hand but did not reach forward to accept it. He looked into the Captain's eyes and came to attention again. He said nothing.

The hand remained extended in the space between them. Then a slow look of understanding came into Captain Benjamin Posee's eyes. It was followed by a momentary expression of unconcealed pain.

"Dismissed, Corporal." he said softly.

Jack wheeled and left.

As he stepped through the door Kendrick looked at Sergeant Scott. Scott's face reflected a bemused smile.

"Got that DD214 and mustering out voucher now?"

Scott handed him both. "DD 214 sets you free. Voucher is for $247.35. That's $152.15 to L.A., a month's pay, and four days of unused leave. Don't spend it all in one place."

"Thanks, Scotty. Much as anything I appreciate your keeping me sane."

Jack extended his hand and Scott stood. They clasped hands, enjoying the moment. Jack stepped away and picked up his cover.

"So long, Scott."

"So long, Beach Bum."

As Jack stepped out the office door he found himself not turning to the right and the exit down the hall, but to his left.

He knew what he intended though he'd never thought of it. Four steps brought him to a door on the right of the hallway marked, "Master Gunnery Sergeant Louis Roundtree." He knocked.

"Come!"

Jack opened the door and stepped in. "You got a minute for me, Top?"

Roundtree looked up, removed his wire-rimmed glasses, and, with just a hint of a smile showing at the corners of his eyes, said, "Just a minute or two, Kendrick."

Jack took the few steps across the room and stood looking down at the luminous black face he so admired. His cover was held in both hands turning slowly in his fingers.

"That your DD214 sticking out the top of your shirt pocket?"

Jack nodded. "May I ask you a question, Top?"

"Fire."

"Why didn't you throw the book at me, Top? Why'd you let me off so easy?"

Roundtree looked straight into his eyes, into his soul. It was all Jack could do not to blink. Finally, the penetration left the gaze and Roundtree's eyes and lips broke into a smile.

"You've got a long drive home don't you, Kendrick?"

Jack nodded again.

"And as best I can judge a long and maybe happy life before you."

No response was requested or required, so Jack gave none.

"I'll let you ponder that, Kendrick. When you figure it out, you'll have something worth knowing."

Roundtree looked down at the paper before him, picked up his glasses, put them on, and went back to his work.

Jack stood unsatisfied and transfixed.

Without looking up Roundtree added, "That will be all."

Jack turned slowly and made the three steps to the door take as long as possible, hoping for more. He opened the door slowly and stepped out. As he turned to close it Roundtree looked up.

"*Semper Fi,* Marine."

When Jack reached the van it started the first time he tried. He drove west.

IT was only ten A.M., but as he looked down the grade toward Kingman and the desert floor, heat was already rising in waves that would be creating mirages before noon. He'd left Albuquerque at midnight, trying to nurse the dying Corvair van across the desert. He'd used five of the six quarts of oil he'd started with—he'd added the fifth in Flagstaff—but now the more critical problem had become the radiator. He wasn't certain if the core was coated with residue of hard water or the thermostat was going bad, but crossing the Llana Estacado in eastern New Mexico it had gotten so hot he'd had to turn the heater on full bore to bleed heat from the engine. Given it was 100 degrees outside without the heater blazing, Jack wasn't sure which was going to expire first, him or the olive drab Corvair Greenbrier van he'd bought from the O-Club when they surveyed it.

So he'd stayed the day in Albuquerque in the shade of a pepper tree at a park and tried to sleep in the heat, and left at midnight. In another twenty minutes he'd have dropped the 5,000 feet from Flagstaff and be on the desert floor. Another sixty miles and he'd cross the Colorado River and be home— sorta. At least he'd be in California, with a long three hundred miles to go across the Sonora desert before he reached home.

But he didn't think the van would make more than sixty miles in the heat. He wouldn't push it past Kingman. Today he'd hole up there and take off again at midnight for the sprint home. Kingman would be fifteen or twenty degrees warmer than Albuquerque. No chance to sleep there without air conditioning.

Motel 6 here I come.

Jack eased off the gas pedal and coasted down the exit ramp from I-40 into Kingman.

Old Route 66—the Mother Road.

THE desk clerk gave him what he needed—a cheap but clean, air-conditioned room, directions to an ice plant, and an eleven-thirty P.M. wake-up call. After getting the room, Jack filled the gas tank and bought one more quart of oil, just in case. He drove to a Denny's to stuff himself on pancakes and eggs and then sought out the ice plant.

"How late you open?" he asked.

"We close at seven P.M., but you can buy a ten-pound bag for ten cents from the machine anytime," the kid answered.

"I'll need a twenty-five-pound block at midnight. How do I get it?"

"That will cost you a quarter in the slot of that machine." He pointed to the metal-clad shack at the edge of the parking lot. "Late night party?"

"Late night drive," Jack answered.

— . —

IT was just after midnight when Jack pulled up to the ice house again. It was still ninety degrees. He'd slept, at least rested, all day and stuffed himself again with pancakes and eggs just a few minutes ago. He also made certain he had a quarter when he left the restaurant. He parked so the passenger-side door was a few steps from the ice machine and stepped out of the van.

Just as the kid had said, a quarter in the slot rewarded him with the satisfying sound of a twenty-five-pound block of ice sliding out of the ice house and onto the catch rail at his knees. He picked it up and quickly stepped to the open van door. Once there he placed the block on the front floor in the middle, so it was just below the heater vent.

At least I won't have to worry about water pooling on the floorboard. It will run out those rust holes as fast as it melts.

As Jack pulled back onto the Interstate, he rolled up his window and pulled the ventilator open. He was rewarded instantly with a cool breeze as the air rushed over the ice block before reaching his feet.

Now for just five or six very boring hours and I'll be where I want.

AT six A.M. he'd watched the sun come up in his rear view mirror, and as he approached the four-level interchange that was ground-zero for downtown Los Angeles, he watched it flood in golden hue from the top to the bottom of the twenty-seven stories of City Hall. Bill Ballance's voice on the radio welcomed him back like an old friend.

"Boys and girls out there in radio-land, let me start your day with one that lingers on the charts. Here's Mama Cass and her pals with their signature song."

All the leaves are brown
And the sky is gray.
I've been for a walk
On a winter's day.

Sing along now, Jack. Belt it out.

I'd be safe and warm
If I was in L.A.

BAM! The van jolted like it had been hit.

"What the fuck!" he screamed at no one.

But I'm still rolling. No acceleration but I'm still rolling. Steering has no hydraulics, but I can force it.

Decelerating rapidly, Jack forced his way to the right and coasted to a stop on the shoulder of the Harbor Freeway just south of downtown. He stepped out looking at almost no traffic on his side but the early rush already filling the north-bound lanes. As he walked to the rear of the van where Jack expected to see collision damage there was none.

Engine? What the hell could have caused that?

He opened the rear doors of the van, pushed the almost empty case of oil forward, picked up his sea bag and pulled it out and dropped it on the ground. He opened the engine housing compartment on the floor of the van. And there it was.

The generator, normally mounted at the top, was gone. Well, it was there, but not mounted. It had broken loose and fallen. As it fell it had snapped the belt and pulled it along. And the loose belt had pulled everything else with it—the carburetor and spark plug lines mostly pulled out and wrapped in a ball around the generator, then slowly swinging back and forth below the engine and above the pavement.

Jack shut the rear door of the van. He patted the quarter panel of the van as he walked around to the passenger side door.

"Thanks, Baby. All I asked was you get me back here. You were faithful."

He rummaged through the glove-box until he found it—the title. A bit more rummaging and he found a pencil. Jack turned the title over and saw a signature block labeled, "Former Owner/Seller" and scrawled "Jack Kendrick."

He set the executed title on the driver's seat, checked to make certain the keys were still in the ignition, and then walked to the rear and retrieved his sea bag. He swung it up over his shoulder and slowly stepped off the highway and into the ice plant that covered the slope down to the streets of L.A. He sang loudly as he went.

I'd be safe and warm
if I was in L.A.
California Dreamin'...."

— · —